MEASURING UP

Measuring Up

...She lay on her back, her rear nestled where the high portion of the chaise met the cushion, calves resting on the furniture back, legs crossed at the ankles. Her head was turned the direction opposite him, as if she were staring out the floor-to-ceiling windows. Her golden hair fanned on the velvet, closest arm dangled toward the floor, and the other stretched above her head. Breasts were more visible than the stars on the clearest south Florida night. And she wasn't wearing panties.

He dropped his bundles on the floor.

She looked toward the ruckus.

His pencil case had opened on impact, and he bent to gather his media. "Sorry. I didn't expect... You surprised me."

"Is this all right?"

"I thought you'd be on your tummy."

She yawned, stretched the entire length of her body, flexed and pointed her toes. Apparently, she'd found her comfort zone. "You already drew my back."

"Just a small part of your back." He was about to close the pencil case but remembered he'd need one to draw with. He selected one and glanced up at her.

She'd already looked back toward the window.

"Sure you don't want a blanket?"

"I'm fine."

Yes, you are...

MEASURING UP

BY

PENNY DAWN

AMBER QUILL PRESS, LLC
http://www.amberquill.com

MEASURING UP
AN AMBER QUILL PRESS BOOK

Amber Quill Press, LLC
http://www.amberquill.com

Layout and Formatting provided by: ElementalAlchemy.com

PUBLISHED IN THE UNITED STATES OF AMERICA

For the man who loves me and our beautiful girls.

ACKNOWLEDGMENTS

All Ptaszeks, Norinis, Gunthers, Steffens, and extensions thereof: If you thought trashy novels and thong undies were inappropriate Christmas gifts among family...hold on tight; I'm about to get racy. Thanks for grounding me and watching me fly.

To my brother, Ken, and my daddy: thanks for hopping over at the drops of many hats to help me put my home back together, once I'd taken it apart. Many lessons learned...and they've gone into this book.

Muchos gracias *to my mother, Star, for teaching me everything I know about making homes out of houses, and to my sister, Chelsey, for the constant rotation of furniture between us. Where's that damn chaise longue?*

To the Sassy-n-Saucy Jacki King, I extend my utmost appreciation for your paving the path with yellow brick. I'm home at last, and there's no place like it.

Mr. Montgomery, thanks for the extra depth in regards to all things masculine. You're an attentive audience—always. Business is a pleasure, n'est-ce pas?

Many thanks to my cold readers, Li'l Kristin, Mary, and the goddess, Angela. Hopefully, I've managed to warm you with my words from time to time. Ooh la la.

Without my critique group at Seton Hill University—Jillicious, Meline, Renee, and Kiki—I'd be writing soft-core porn. Thanks also to all faculty, staff, and students of SHU, especially mentor fantastica, Leslie Davis Guccione. Your support is incomparable.

Much gratitude to Danny Reese, whose knowledge of framing for Custom Homebuilder of the Year 2000 pushed this story beyond the average boy-meets-girl-and-falls. Keep your balance up there.

Thanks to Suzanne Forster, for inscribing luck with her autograph.

Shannon Hollis, you're an inspiration to all of us. Enough said.

Finally, age-old and long-overdue thanks to Jerry Kurszewski for introducing this little girl from across the street to magical Fort Lauderdale. Alas, you're forgiven for leaving me in wait at the airport.

CHAPTER 1

Nicolette Jeanne Paige. Vixen personified.

"It can't be." Ty Carmichael peered through second-story stud walls under construction at the approaching woman, all curves with long, shapely legs. A few steps ahead of his boss, she paused at the Diamond Custom Homes sign and slid her sunglasses from the bridge of her nose to the crown of her head, into a mass of long, curly hair the color of spun gold. It was Nicki, all right. In the flesh.

He turned to the group of five laborers breathing stagnant Fort Lauderdale air—and doing little else. "Big guy's here." Had he mentioned the gorgeous girl accompanying Ray Diamond, the crew might have flinched, if only to catch a glimpse of her curvaceous hips.

Damn it, she'd been pretty enough back home as a kid; where did she get off filling out like that?

With a dirty hand, he shifted his favorite baseball cap, boasting the Chicago Bulls' Threepeat, and started toward her, bounding down the rickety, job site stairs.

Despite her ridiculously high-heeled sandals, Nicki easily negotiated the South Florida loam of the job site. An indiscernible air emanated from her like a halo of light around a saint—that is, if a religious icon wore a low-rise, denim mini skirt—and when she drew nearer, a smile touched her lips, rich in color, like milk chocolate. Wow. To see that mouth devouring an ice cream cone...

"Found this wandering around the airport." Ray Diamond hitched his chin in Nicki's direction. "Yours?"

1

I wish. Ty glanced at three large suitcases perched on the curb and swiped his hands against his worn jeans. "Not lately. But I'll take her."

With a raised eyebrow, she pecked a kiss at the corner of his lips and withdrew, leaving a raspberry-vanilla aroma in her wake. "Hi, stranger." Her voice seduced like a tall, cool drink in the sweltering sun, and disregarding the heat, hair perked on the back of his neck, as if she'd breathed a whisper into his ear. Why wasn't she wearing her engagement ring?

Without a break in his stride, Ray whisked past. "How's it going in there? They still giving you trouble about your designer tie?"

Couture and nail guns didn't usually mix, but when Ty had presented his plans as the architect, he'd never dreamed Ray would consider him for superintendent on site. "They're getting used to me."

"I'll see if I can light a fire for you." Ray climbed the construction stairs into the house, where the crew began to stir. At least the guys *looked* busy, if only for the boss' benefit.

Unable to look away from his visitor, Ty chucked her under the chin. "You said you might come, but you never confirmed."

She twirled a curl around a delicate finger and swept her glance over the job site. "I left several messages this morning."

He pulled the cell phone from his pocket. Five missed calls. "I didn't hear it ring. How long were you waiting?"

"I called your office." She slipped her left foot from the sandal and, with a hand on his bicep for balance, fiddled with a ring on her fourth toe. "Ray and I got to talking, and he picked me up. I'm fine."

She certainly was. He tried not to look at the white, sleeveless blouse, too sheer, with one-button-too-many unfastened at her cleavage—or at the hint of lace beneath it, beckoning him to peer more closely. And that stretchy skirt hiking higher up her thighs threatened to raise more than his eyebrows.

With a scorching desire burning hotly, he longed to pull her into his arms. She was old enough now—twenty-three—and their eight-year age difference was now a non-issue. But sixteen years of history loomed over his shoulder like a watchman. *Hands off. She's the little girl from across the street.*

She stood a safe distance away, gazing at the monstrous frame of the house. "Quite a monument to someone's ego, don't you think?"

"It's a specification house, built for sale. No ego involved, unless you count mine. I volunteered to oversee the whole project." He glanced over his shoulder at the sudden whirlwind of activity inside the

2

structure. "I'm aiming for a Key Award, and if my crew would execute a task—just one—without questioning me, I might earn the nomination."

She shifted her brown eyes toward the lush, green palm trees on the south side of the site and then to the ocean in the distance. "Breathtaking view."

"You've got that right."

The late afternoon sun darted through her hair, and with a rush of Atlantic breeze, a tad cool for late April, her clothing hugged her curves, and her nipples distended beneath her shirt.

"I feel like I've been here before." A windswept curl fell over one eye. "Do you ever feel that way?" She brushed the tendril from her forehead. "Comfortable? At home somewhere you've never been before?"

"I've been home here for two years, but comfortable? Not even close. Too much pressure to prove my worth on the job site." And too much anxiety regarding Mandy Washington's pending paternity suit, but Ty wasn't about to open that closet door in plain view of the one girl he'd never disappointed. He wiped sweat from under the bill of his cap.

Behind him, the *thwack* of nail guns floated down from the second story, where the crew was framing interior walls. Better late than never. But amid the hullabaloo, he felt content now that an element of his past, a reminder of home, stood close enough to touch.

The perfume of a nearby jasmine vine mingled with Nicki's scent as if she'd sprouted there. And like the natural beauty of South Florida's landscape, she commanded attention. In Chicago, he'd never allowed himself the pleasure, but suddenly, he imagined what she might look like nude.

The picture in his mind, so vivid, so sensual, hovered like a scintillating daydream: her ivory skin illuminated with the stream of a single spotlight in an otherwise black studio; her eyes closed, face lifted to heaven, arms outstretched, one knee slightly bent, and toes curled against an ebony pedestal.

He'd long ago taken to sketching homes instead of women, but Ty longed to record Nicki's figure, to capture the definition of *woman* for his private archives.

"Crack out your portfolio." She tilted her head in a way that made her look coy and enticing all at the same time. "One look at your work, and they'll realize you know a thing or two about custom homes."

"Optimistic." He hooked his thumb under the bracket of the tape measure clipped at his left hip and pulled it out a few inches. "But I'm a white-collar in a blue-collar field. That portfolio sets me apart." The tape recoiled with a zip. "They hate me."

"It's their loss then. Who could hate you?"

"You want a list? I'm way behind schedule on a project I proposed, that Ray didn't want to touch. And since Mandy quit, I owe him a secretary. How you sweet-talked him into taking time out of his day to pick you up, I'll—"

"Are you going to show me this house or what?" She tossed a curl over her shoulder and tapped her toes against the dirt.

All his headaches waned when he studied those sexy feet.

The urge to unravel her secrets—and God help him, her clothing—boiled beneath his skin, evoking an innate desire to create. And this craving would not likely be sated with a hammer and nails. "Nicki Jeanne."

"Yeah?" Her gorgeous head turned toward him, her blonde curls bounced against her sun-starved shoulders and her glossed lips parted.

God, those lips. Had they always been that full, that luscious? "Why aren't you wearing your engagement ring?"

She looked back to the ocean. "I came to my senses."

"What happened?"

She crossed her arms over her breasts. "It's personal."

"So is your body, but you share *that* with strangers."

Her eyes narrowed, full of fire. "They're students."

"Students you don't know."

"We're not having this conversation again."

"Well, you're going to talk about something."

"I don't share my body with strangers." She frowned, and her lower lip hung heavy for a split second. "They draw me, and that's the end of it."

"You take your clothes off for money. Not everyone sees past that. If I'd been there, no way in hell would I have let you take that job."

"I beg your pardon?" Her frown deepened. "*Let* me?"

"When my father didn't offer you a full-time position at the end of your internship, you should've come to me for help. I could've pushed him for your letter of commendation and helped you find a job in the right industry. That is, in case you've forgotten, something related to interior design."

"You were too busy running away from home to notice, but the

4

moment you left, you hardly had a leg to stand on."

"I'll have more than a leg up, once I win the Key."

"Ah, the coveted Key. What every custom homebuilder wants. Slim chance of that happening without the respect of your crew, don't you think?"

"I'm not stopping at the Key, Nicki Jeanne." Ty's tape measure zipped. "I'll pull Custom Homebuilder of the Year right out from under my father's mahogany desk. I want it all."

"That makes two of us." She perched her hands on her hips, fingers framing her belly button.

"What'll it take to keep you clothed and in a showroom?"

"Who says I want to be? Somewhere along the way, I grew up without your supervision, and I make my own decisions. Accept that."

"Modeling in the buff is not growing up."

She turned her back to him, reached into the pocket of her clinging skirt, and pulled out her cell phone. She dialed, put the phone to her ear, and walked toward the house.

"Walk away. Real grown up, Nicki."

His cell phone rang, and Nicki's name flashed in the caller ID screen. "What?" he answered.

"I'm tired, Ty."

"I'm right behind you, for God's sake." He plucked at the tape measure again.

"Look, I don't have the energy for your judgment right now. Not about my job and not about my life. And one of these days, you have to stop worrying about me."

"How can I not worry? You called at two in the morning, hysterical, and suddenly, you're here."

"Have you ever taken advantage of a nude model?"

"This isn't about me, Nicki."

"You've taken advantage of plenty of women, and not only models, Ty. When it comes to me, you're the king of double standards." Phone at her ear, she paused at a portable workbench, where he'd laid out the blueprints. "You haven't always earned your paychecks swinging hammers. Once upon a time you were an architect, who wouldn't dream of sweating."

"We've been over this before. Several times."

"Let's review, shall we?"

"I like working with my hands." He'd always been good with his hands in art school, molding clay into a woman's back, sketching a woman's eyes in charcoal… And his hands and Nicki's body could be a winning combination.

"Still there?"

Oh, hell, he hadn't been listening. "Yeah."

"I asked if you were happy. You feel creative every day, don't you?" She flipped a page, her slender fingers floating over the plans. "You're using your three-dimensional mind, and it fulfills you."

"It might, someday. If I'm nominated—"

"Without inspiration, there can be no creativity."

He drew in a long breath and walked toward her, wanting to reach and sustain her.

"Think of me as an inspiration," she said. "Instead of as a nude."

"I think of you as both, Nicki Jeanne."

Her gaze met his through the frame of a window; she looked like a schoolgirl awaiting a serenade.

His heart galloped, and his cheeks warmed. "I don't doubt you awaken dead souls everywhere. Who wouldn't want to be alone in a studio with you?"

Her jaw descended a fraction of an inch.

"I mean…" Only twenty feet and a maze of rough-framed walls stood between them. Why wasn't he walking faster? "I'm sure you're a great subject. In my undergrad years, I drew chubby girls. And even they turned me on sometimes, but you…You in a studio would be…" *Nothing short of riveting.*

Her quick, flirty tongue swept across her lips. "Ty, are you saying you'd like to draw me?"

Absolutely. Right here, right now. "I'm saying you should keep your clothes on." He entered the house. "If taking them off compromises you."

"The people who draw me don't look at my body as something they want to romp with. You know, maybe if you draw me, you'll stop judging me."

"I'm not judging you." He paced around the workbench and stopped before her. The high heels, coupled with the short skirt, made her seem leggier than five-seven, and it took determined control to refrain from leering at her thighs. He ended the call, licking his suddenly arid lips. "I'm looking out for you."

"Over twelve hundred miles?" She snapped her phone shut. "Thanks, but no thanks."

"Someone has to." He raised her chin with one hand, and dragged a finger along her soft skin.

She blinked up at him, heat ever-present in her tawny eyes, and her breasts rose emphatically with a deep breath. "I can't marry him. I can't."

Answer her. He lost concentration when he watched her mouth move. Those lips might be the death of him. *Answer her!* "It's all right. You don't have to."

"I thought I was doing the right thing, but…" When she shook her head, her satiny cheek caressed his rough hand. "Nothing could've been more wrong."

He swept a lock of hair from her temple and secured it under his thumb. "What did he do? Just tell me what he—"

"It doesn't matter, does it?"

She was right. When her eyes shone with such intensity, nothing else mattered. Not the Key Award. Not Mandy's baby. And certainly not her ex-fiancé in Chicago.

Nothing compared to finding one's purpose in life, and suddenly, he'd found his: to make her the happiest, most satisfied woman on the face of the earth. *Impossible. Stop thinking about it. Stop, stop, stop.*

Her tongue traveled over her bottom lip. "I'd love a man to be passionate about me, I'll admit it," she said. "I deserve it."

"Don't say anything else."

"But no one should assume that just because a girl happens to be naked during her day job—"

"Stop."

*   *   *

His strong hands tightened around her arms, and she felt very small next to him. Her heart raced when she gauged the expression in his sparkling, bright blue eyes. Animal attraction, desire. Why was he looking at her like that? "Ty, I—"

"Don't say anything else. Please." He released her, stepped back, and stumbled into a pile of two-by-fours.

She grasped his hand to steady him, and although he'd already regained his composure and balance by the time they touched, a wave of heat washed over her on contact. He blinked down at her, his eyes smoldering.

A refreshing breeze whispered against her skin, and she stepped closer to his muscled body, bronzed to a glistening, sweating gold in the Florida sun.

One massive, callused hand brushed against the small of her back and gave a gentle tug on her hair. His eyes pooled to the brightest blue. "Nicki, I..."

She shook her head and caught a breath in her throat. No time for words. *My God.* She was going to fall for him. Not in the sense of the familiar schoolgirl crush she'd always harbored, but irrationally, hopelessly. Would he catch her?

He smelled of virility, of a man consumed with indecent thoughts and sexual energy. Understated aftershave. Hard work and muscle.

"Nicki Jeanne." He brushed the rough pads of his fingers against her back.

Not every man had hands like his. Some didn't know what to do with them, but this one probably did.

Her legs parted and blood rushed to their apex. She brought a hand to his heated cheek, memorizing the flex of his jaw, and she drew in even closer. If she could turn malleable from his stare, what would happen when Ty—

That's Ty. She pulled away her hand.

The beating of his heart reverberated against her chest. "Oh, my God, Ty."

Long, dark lashes fluttered over his indigo eyes, and he retracted.

"Ty..."

He leaned heavy against the workbench and, with a deep sigh, nodded at the blueprints. "So what do you think?"

"About what?"

"The house."

Did he honestly expect her to analyze a plan? Now? She pushed an annoying, stray tendril from her forehead and leaned in next to him, flushed and disoriented. She felt the dampness in her panties and her heart continued to race. *Focus, Nicki. Focus.* "Clean. Organized site."

"No, I mean the layout. Something about the traffic flow between the kitchen and dining room...it's not right."

"Why? What about it isn't—" She looked up from the plans.

He was staring at her; a concentrated squint revealed tiny lines at the corners of his eyes. "What happened last night?"

Should she tell him about the edge of the granite countertop digging into the small of her back and the duct tape meant to imprison her? Should she reveal the teeth marks on her hip?

"Nicki?"

Too humiliating. All of it. She turned back to the plans. "Push the

8

plumbing back into the laundry room. You'll get an extra foot in the butler's pantry." She pulled the tape measure from his belt and stretched the yellow tape across the plans, scaling. "About sixty-six inches that way. Sufficient. More open."

"You aren't going to tell me."

She released the tape measure, met his steady gaze, and glanced at his dingy cap, testimony to the Bulls' long-dead dynasty. How long was he planning on wearing that disgusting, faded hat anyway?

As if he could read her thoughts, he yanked it off his head, raked through an unruly mess of sun-glinted hair, and shoved the hat back on. "You want refuge, Nicki? I'll it give to you, but in return, I think I deserve to know."

Well, that was probably true, but was he entitled to know everything? It was personal business—*her* personal business. And like her posing, there was nothing he could do to change it.

"I'll listen. Without judgment, I promise." His eyes mellowed to a blue as tranquil as the summer Atlantic, melting, pleading.

She wouldn't deny those eyes a damn thing. Never could. "Do you remember the Delassandro Farmhouse rehab in Lake Forest? Gorgeous on the outside, desecrated on the inside?"

"Mmm-hmm." His right eyebrow peaked.

"Have you ever felt as ruined as that house?"

*   *   *

The expression in her eyes caused his heart to beat like a bass drum. He wanted to look away, but the sight of her held his attention.

She looked even prettier consumed with deep emotion, and while he knew it was the last thing she needed, he longed to kiss her. But not here. Not with Ray Diamond and five tradesman due to fly down the stairs at any minute. Hell, the thought shouldn't have entered his head at all, considering what she'd always been to him.

"I'm not a little girl anymore."

"Obviously."

"Why do you never assume I can take care of myself? Your father's refusal to back me, my posing...you can't change any of it."

"My father had no right to turn his back on you."

"Funny, he said the same thing about you."

"I can't work for my father, can't stand to be anywhere near him. I had no choice but to leave."

Her tempting lower lip sagged, and for a moment, she looked like

9

the pink-clad, seven-year-old girl he'd met at the mailbox sixteen years ago.

"You were such a pretty kid, you know that?"

She rolled her eyes. "Thanks."

"But you're a knock-out woman, Nicki, and the fact you don't even know it... Believe me, you don't need that pedestal, or your posing, to prove you're beautiful. I wish you believed that."

"That type of faith is impossible to have."

"Anyone on overtime tomorrow?" Ray stomped down the stairs, his inquiry met with groans from the crew following him.

Ty stepped back, cushioning their bodies with three feet of air.

"You've got plumbers on proposed agenda in two weeks," Ray said. "You're not even under roof. Less than half the walls are in up there. You're behind schedule."

"Only by a week or so," Ty said over his shoulder, reluctant to take his eyes off her. "I can make it up working weekends."

"I'll give you a hand." Nicki grasped the bound edge of the plans in one hand and his tape measure in the other. She started toward the butler's pantry.

Her heels clicked against the plywood decking, and Ty suspected the five pairs of eyes behind him were glued to her swaying rear end. She dropped the plans to the floor, straightened them with a toe, and unrolled the tape measure along the wall.

"More than the plumbing congests this part of the house," she said. "Got a pencil?"

Ty reached to his back pocket, but Montalvo, the crew's journeyman framer, was already at her side, arms folded over his bulky chest, watching her sketch on a stud.

"You need a way out of the dining room," she said, "as well as in. You can't rely on one passage in a house of this magnitude; party guests will tangle with the catering crew, and...there." She tapped the pencil against her sketch. "You need something like this."

Ty shouldered past the journeyman for a closer look. She'd reconfigured a storage closet into a secondary pass-through with a wet bar. She'd solved, in mere seconds, the problem that had nagged at him for weeks.

"We have to stay on budget, so overtime's gonna be limited." Ray made his way toward the door. "Take it while it's offered."

"Hey, thanks again for the ride," Nicki said.

As Ray whistled a goodbye, he held up a stiff palm in lieu of waving.

Ty turned to his crew. "I'll be here tomorrow, working for free. But it's time-and-a-half if anyone wants to join me."

*   *   *

Ty held her arm with a rugged hand as they walked over the uneven terrain of the job site. In Chicago, his hands had been suave, executive, but his were the hands of a laborer now, invigorating against her skin.

"There's a sweatshirt on the front seat." He released her arm at the roadside and turned to stow her luggage in the backseat of his car. "Wear it."

A pair of crew members drove off in a cloud of dust.

"I'm fine."

"You'll be cold on the road with the top down."

"Do you remember what it feels like to be cold?" She leaned against his vintage Ford Mustang, slipped off her sandals, and clapped dirt from the heels. "It was twenty-seven degrees back home this morning. It snowed last week."

"Humor me, all right? Wear it."

She wiggled her feet back into her shoes. "How about humoring me? Let me drive."

"Not today." He dragged a finger along the hood, rounding the vehicle, a 1964½ model, painted to match the original factory color of Pillow Yellow. The only car ever to win a Tiffany Award for design. "Not today" was every day.

"What is it with you and this pile of scrap metal?" She climbed into the delicious convertible and relaxed against the white vinyl upholstery.

"Careful. She'll hear you."

"Heaven forbid."

"Jealous of the old gal?" He turned the key, but the car only whinnied.

"Hardly." She pulled the sweatshirt over her head, inhaling the masculine scent lingering in the threads.

"Come on, Betty." He turned the key again. The motor sputtered but soon died. With the next attempt, the engine turned over, and he grinned. "Good girl." He patted the dashboard and inched away from the curb. "Good girl."

"So is it just me? Do you let anyone else drive her?"

"You learned how to drive stick on Betty, so I don't want to hear it."

"You may have taught me how to shift, but you never let me drive."

He steered away from the treasure of the ocean-view lot and turned toward rows of massive homes. "Hey, I appreciate your input back there with the butler's pantry."

"My pleasure."

"Was it?" He turned onto Highway A1A, meeting her eyes for a fraction of a second. "You're good at what you do. You see things in a blueprint..."

Here we go.

"There's no reason you should be doing...you know, what you do."

"I suppose my wanting to do 'what I do' isn't reason enough." She stared at the storefronts along A1A, outdoor cafés muddled with patrons across from Fort Lauderdale Beach. Spanish moss and bright yellow flowers sprouted from window boxes. Even the drabbest stucco looked alive surrounded with green palms and fuchsia hibiscus.

"Do me a favor." He twitched a smile. "Keep your clothes on while you're here." His glance lingered a few moments longer than normal. Did he just look at her thighs? "You concentrate on doing that, and together we can win this Key. Maybe even Custom Homebuilder of the Year."

God, had anyone ever dared to say *no* to that smile?

"Of course, you'll have to work on a tan, too." He nudged her with his golden elbow. "I'll bet you glow in the dark, don't you?"

"I can probably arrange some beach time."

"Shouldn't be too difficult. We're less than a mile from the ocean."

"Really? How do you get anything done?"

"Motivation." He turned west on Las Olas Boulevard. "I live in a house I can barely afford."

She clucked her tongue. "Sucker for a sweet pile of bricks, aren't you?"

"It's stucco." He lifted a few fingers from the gear shift.

She accepted his subtle invitation and slipped her hand under his. Shifting Betty and holding his hand—both comforting, reminiscent of old days.

"This is New River," he said. "Part of the intracoastal waterway, where I live."

"You live on the water?"

"On a channel really. A series of canals connect the intracoastal, and the streets are small peninsulas between them. It's like Venice in America."

The hum of the motor rose through the gear shift to her palm. Calluses brushed against her knuckles. He nodded to the right. "That's Lago Balboa."

Green, thriving foliage.

"And to the left, Sunset Lake. I draw there sometimes."

"You're drawing again?"

"Not women, and definitely not nude women. Just…things."

They downshifted and steered Betty over a small bridge to the north onto Isle of Venice Drive, and parked under a carport covering a pink stone driveway.

She stood in the car, hands gripping the windshield, and studied the house looming before her, Mediterranean in architectural style. While larger than the neighboring structures, its size wasn't overwhelming or overbearing, due to the shallow pitch of the roof and the quaint, covered porch wrapping around the east and south sides.

The stucco was pale yellow, suspiciously close to the color of Betty, and arched, mint green shutters framed the windows. A black wrought iron railing caged the half-moon ledge of a single, square window high in the gable.

"Charming," she whispered, climbing out of the car.

"Don't draw any conclusions yet." Ty led her onto the porch. "I know you like things a certain way. Orderly. And the entrails of this shack are anything but."

"I'm sure it's fine."

"Far from it, really. If I'd known you were coming, I might have put some of it back together for you, but…" He pushed the door wide open to reveal raw studs, drywall dust. Plywood floors. "Enter at your own risk."

She took a tentative step inside. "It's…" Filthy came to mind. She looked up, down, around. Half the house seemed to be gutted without rhyme or reason. Unlivable. "It's huge."

"Yeah, it's big for just me, but it was too good a deal to pass up. My neighbor Verna needed the money after her husband died." He shoved the keys into his pocket. "Come on. I'll show you around."

She didn't know if she could stand to see much more, but she followed him through a labyrinth of two-by-fours, past a sanded-down staircase.

"Here's a bathroom." When he scooted a sheet of quarter-inch plywood aside, he revealed a tiny powder room beneath the stairs, wallpapered in 1970's olive velour stripes. "It's workable, but not entirely private. I bid on a vintage door—gotta love eBay, right?—but until it arrives, this'll have to make do." He knocked on the plywood.

She shrugged. "Does the plumbing work?"

"Yeah, if you jiggle the handle and hold the flapper."

"Quite a bit of effort for a flush, don't you think?"

"I'll get around to finishing things. I guess I started with the outside, and I'm working my way in."

Just like a man. "So what's your décor?"

"Décor?"

"Mediterranean, to fit the style? Nautical, to fit the locale?"

"And you don't consider yourself a designer?" His smile became a snicker.

"Say art deco, and I'll smack you."

He flipped his dirty cap off with one hand, smoothed his hair with the other, and placed the hat back on his head. "I don't know."

"You don't know?"

"No, I thought I'd see where the project takes me."

Worse than art deco. "You mean you don't have plans?"

"Sure, I have plans."

"Let's see them."

"They're all up here." He tapped his temple.

"You're kidding, right?"

"You should've seen the place, Nicki Jeanne. Orange shag carpeting. Wrought iron painted white. It was itching for a sledge hammer."

"You'd rather live like this?"

"Well, yeah. Unlike you, I just…go with the flow. I've never been very good at plans."

"You're better than good. Who blocked out the house you're working on now?"

"That's different. When it comes to structure and layout, I can hold my own. But hit me with a question on detail—motifs, period décor— and I'm clueless. Ray can't afford an interior consultant, so if you're going to be around for a while, you can help me win that Key."

"You don't need my help. And who says I'm sticking around?"

"Three suitcases and a carry-on?" He flashed a quick smile. "I'm open to suggestions. For this place and the job site."

She wandered farther down the hall, stepping over a tangle of disconnected electrical whips and wires. "Where do you cook in all this chaos?"

"On the grill."

"Okay, where do you store food?"

"In the refrigerator."

"So you have a kitchen."

"Part of a kitchen anyway. Want to see it?"

"I don't know. Do I?"

"Would you rather skip it and go straight upstairs?"

Her glance caught his. "Do you say that to all the girls?"

He chuckled. "There's a livable room up there. Intact. Untouched. Where you can sleep."

A livable room. *One* room. "Just one?"

"The rest of the bedrooms are kind of in pieces. I wasn't expecting out-of-towners. I mean, who's going to visit—my family?"

"If I take your room, where are you going to sleep?"

He swiped sweat from his cheek with the shrug of a shoulder. "We've shared a bed before, right? I can be good until I slap another room together." He kicked at a lump of construction dust. "I guess I could sleep on the floor. Or on the porch maybe, depending on the heat." He pulled at his tape measure. "The weather, that is."

A distinct silence settled between them. Suddenly Ty, the man famous for encouraging celibacy, seemed to be undressing her with his eyes.

The heat of his gaze covered her like a hot mist, and the lingering memory of the prelude to his aborted kiss at the job site rushed through her. She didn't dare move a muscle, for fear he might look away, and she felt beautiful under his scrutiny, as if she'd been thirsting for it for years. Powerful. Intense.

He pulled at his tape measure, and the click of its retraction echoed in the demolished hallway. "I need a shower."

CHAPTER 2

Ty wrapped a black towel around his waist, secured it, and opened the bathroom door. Sun-bleached hair dripped cold water onto his shoulders. He hadn't had a haircut in four months. Nothing would shock his father more, except perhaps finding Nicolette Paige in South Florida—and asleep in his son's bed.

A white, lacy brassiere tangled in his toes, and he bent to pick it up. He'd seen enough of them to recognize its design. Glorious Collection, an unlined demi. A bra designed to lift and separate, enhance cleavage, and inveigle men to stare from worlds away.

Well, it certainly worked.

He looked to his bed, where entwined with basic white linens, Nicki slept. The bed was as rumpled as if she'd been rolling around in it—and not necessarily alone—for hours.

They'd slept side-by-side once, only because beds were a precious commodity in his sister's flat, and it had been too bitter cold that New Year's Eve to catch a cab. He hadn't enjoyed the experience; she was a restless sleeper, and her elbows and knees could have been registered as lethal weapons. Maybe the floor was safe for a number of reasons.

He hung her bra on a robe hook in his walk-in closet, dropped his towel, and stepped into sweat shorts. No matter how enticing her lingerie and her body, he intended to keep her clothed, out of studios, and—even if it killed him—out of his bed.

But for whatever reason, she was already in his bed, and even in sleep, she looked ready to be drawn. One arm stretched above her head, the other rested at her waist with fingers flared against her exposed abdomen. Chin up, as if posture were an important element of sleep, and full lips slightly parted.

Sugar and spice and... She was definitely made of all things nice. *Should I draw her?*

Such ambiguity. He didn't agree with her posing for strangers, but he couldn't ignore her position now. He would have to draw fast, before she moved again, but he didn't have a choice. The tableau was too ideal to ignore.

The rays of the setting sun slanted across her stomach, in just the right location, and his sweatshirt bunched under her breasts, displaying an adorable belly button, a deep, oval-shaped inny. The wrinkled top sheet rested at her hips, revealing only a peek at her panties.

If he had his way, he'd remove the sweatshirt from the equation; the pretty picture before him would be entirely white without it. Her panties, the linens, the pale highlights in her hair...even her skin was ivory.

He studied her, starting with her face. Wide eyes, narrow nose. In any light, her cheekbones drew shadows to her square chin and a subdued indentation in it. He wouldn't call it a dimple so much as a slight depression that played nicely off her full bottom lip.

Skip the lips, skip 'em, skip 'em, skip 'em.

Too late. He was already pondering their powers of suction and seduction. The member between his legs perked in interest.

Down, boy.

The hollow at the base of her neck might be a nice place to kiss her. Then again, would any body part not be?

Her breasts. A given, no matter what they looked like, and they were probably unbelievable, with or without the help of the Glorious bra. Her shoulders, the insides of her wrists. Definitely. He wanted to lick her skin right where her hip met her waist, right there, at the convex of an amazing curve, where that little red, moon-shaped mark...

What is that? He drew in closer, knelt onto the bed, and reached for her.

Just in time, she rolled over, barely missing his arm with her knee. He looked out the window. It had been years since he'd drawn a human body, and a body like this—so perfect, so defined—would take a while, even for a practiced artist. He sketched quickly enough to capture geckos on tree limbs, but lizards were lizards. Commonplace. If he saw one, he saw them all. Not so with women.

But he had time enough to seize a small part of her on paper before she awakened. A tiny patch, that's all. Something to tide him over, to satisfy the nagging sensation between his legs. But with so many scrumptious parts, what would he draw first?

The thrilling, provocative curve in her back, just above the flirty dimples, dared him to tickle her rear end. The small of her back: perfect subject matter. And he'd draw it, all right. Every gorgeous inch of it. Blue bruise and all.

He pinched his eyes shut and envisioned her skin creamy and pure, but when he looked again, reality flooded back. Mottles of purple, black, and blue bled malevolence onto her skin. He wasn't breathing, couldn't convince himself to exhale.

While the vision of her full body evidenced the maturity he'd chosen to ignore in Chicago, his vision of her innocence shattered when he viewed the mark on her back. He could no longer deny what he'd known for years. She was no longer the little girl he'd protected from neighborhood bullies, no more the daughter of undeserving parents. She was a woman, alone. And now, assumedly, abused.

Careful not to wake her, he peeled the sheet down, exposing her panties, but he did little more than glance at them, however alluring. He stared at a horizontal bruise spanning roughly three inches across the small of her back. A lift of the sweatshirt revealed another small bruise along the spine, aligned with her shoulders.

He wanted to shake her awake, to demand an explanation, but he left the bed instead., shoving his hands through his damp hair, wishing he could erase the marks on her back.

What was he going to do? Consoling her seemed too little, too late, as well as a breach of privacy, considering the way he'd discovered her secret. Until she revealed the problem on her own, he couldn't call her on this. But he *could* do something. He'd finish a bedroom and keep her here. Safe, in the confines of his home.

He pulled a sketchbook out of the top drawer in his second-hand dresser, leafed through pages of palms, beach umbrellas, sailboats, and geckos, and reached for the closest tool—a carpenter's pencil, sharpened in the field earlier that day by razor blade to a fine, square tip.

Deep breath. Concentrate on your subject.

Charcoal would compliment her and pastels would flatter her when he had more time. But for now, graphite would have to do her justice. He guided the pencil over the heavy-weight paper with wide, bold strokes. He blended confidently and shadowed with the pad of his thumb, and she breathed a satisfied sigh in her sleep, as if he had touched her skin instead of the paper on which he drew.

"Hmmmm." What a sound.

He fixated on her back, memorizing the pattern of sunlight on her body. And as far as he was concerned, there was no grander place in the world. Her body made his mattress a posh, four-poster bed.

And, heavens, what he wouldn't give to roll her around on a bed of any caliber, to push his way inside her, to feel her walls drip all around him. He would start slowly and finish with painstaking patience. But deep down, he knew the risk in discovering her intimately. Pleasure wasn't worth the pain of losing her.

With disdain, he rubbed the graphite into the paper, and allowed it to drift and bleed, just like the bruise itself.

Ugly, wrong, evil bruise. The wood of the pencil snagged the paper. He'd worn down the graphite. Fine. He didn't want to draw anymore. But he'd nailed it. His representation could have been a photograph.

He dropped his pencil onto the dresser and his sketch pad into the drawer. He massaged his drawing hand with the other and licked his lips, dividing his attention between her body and the sunset, feeling helpless.

When he'd searched for the father she'd never known was the last time he'd felt as weak. He'd failed, of course, and now, because he couldn't save her from the memory of what had given her those bruises, he was about to fail her again.

A long night lay ahead of him, and despite the tiring day he'd had, he did not want to sleep. More likely, he wouldn't be able to, with the aches and pains of overtime haunting his body, Mandy's baby preying on his mind, and Nicki's condition panging his gut.

He should let her sleep. He should spend the evening with a bottle of beer along the intracoastal shore. He should forget his disrespectful crew and Mandy's pregnancy—and the urge to hunt down a violator in Chicago.

As quietly as he could, he exited the bedroom and walked to the room that would be a kitchen again, if he'd only buckle down and do the work. Just as he opened the refrigerator for a bottle of beer, he heard the front door open.

"Ty?" A southern female voice echoed throughout the lower level. "Hi-lo?"

He grabbed two bottles of beer and darted toward the front of the house.

"Ty? You 'round and about?"

His neighbor, Verna Davis, stood in the foyer, wearing a jade-and-black caftan that hid her well-preserved figure. Tendrils of her long, black hair escaped from a rhinestone clip and draped around her sixty-four-year-old face.

When she saw him, her eyes smiled behind her turquoise-tinted sunglasses. "You just got laid." She tickled the air with two wiggling fingers and chomped ruthlessly on a wad of pink gum.

Ty shook his head and handed her a bottle. "Not exactly."

"You don't 'not exactly' get laid. You either do it, or you don't, and you've got the look of a sexually spent man. No shirt, mussed hair." She glanced at his bare feet. "And, for everything that's decadent about peanut brittle, put some shoes on. You'll step on a nail in this god-forsaken place."

"Yeah, let's go outside."

"So tell me." Verna slid the sunglasses down the bridge of her nose and lowered her voice half a notch, as if she were about to tell a secret. "Who is it this time? I thought you was going to lay low, what with the trouble that secretary's giving you."

"You don't know the half of it." He ushered her out the front door. A balmy breeze danced through his hair, and wind chimes jingled in the distance. *Ah, Florida.*

Verna spread her skirts, sat cross-legged on the sidewalk, and looked up at him with a questioning glance. She sipped the beer and then set it on the walk next to her with a clink.

"What?" Ty asked.

"Details, my boy. And what the *schlotsky* is all over your hands?"

Ty rubbed his hands together. "Graphite."

The gum popped between her teeth. "What you been drawing?"

He sipped his beer, lowered himself to the stoop, and set the bottle aside. "Her." He rested his forearms on his thighs and studied his hands. "I've been drawing her."

"Thought you didn't draw women no more."

"I don't. I didn't…I mean, but she looked so…ready for it."

"Before or after you got her in the sack?"

"What?" He snapped his head up.

"Before or after? Was it drawing her that led you to rolling her in the hay, or the other way 'round?"

With a shrug, Ty smiled again. "What did you need?"

"Need?"

"You came over. What did you need?"

"Oh." She lifted a hand to her hair and tucked a few wild tendrils into the clip. "I saw George again this morning."

"Verna, you didn't see him. He's dead."

"I know, but that don't stop him from sitting there in the sunroom, flipping through my paper before I even read my horoscope."

"What did you do last night?"

"Do? Nothing out of the ordinary, I suppose. The ole biddies and me stoked up a poker game, drank a little whiskey, gossiped a lot."

"Smoke anything?"

"Why? You want some leftovers?"

He shook his head. "Maybe you imagined it. That's what I'm saying."

She shrugged. "I suppose I could've, but why would I? That bastard was sticking his willie-nillie into everything in silk panties before he died. Why would I want to imagine living with him again?"

"Good point."

"I suppose I can't blame him. If I'd have gone first, I sure as glitz would be haunting him right now." She aimed her eyes to hell and clenched her hands into tight fists. "George Davis, you always beat me to the punch."

"If he doesn't scare you—and he doesn't, right?—what do you care if you see him every now and then?"

"It's a creepy feeling to leave one man in bed and see... Hey, speaking of leaving someone in bed..."

Ty laughed. "You never quit."

"You always tell. Why not this time?"

With his opposite thumb, he briskly rubbed graphite from the forefinger of his drawing hand to another digit. "Nothing to tell. It's Nicki, for God's sake."

"Nicki, Nicki, Nicki. Can't keep track of them, big boy. Which one's Nicki?"

"I told you about Nicki—the girl who grew up across the street from me, the one I always looked after."

"The one whose daddy you was trying to track down?"

"That's her."

"I suppose that does complicate things now, doesn't it? You can't very well sack the girly you're always protecting. Can't save her from yourself, once you do."

"I'm tempted, don't get me wrong. But there's a lot going on."

"With that secretary, Mandy."

He nodded. "She showed up at my job site yesterday. The whole crew probably knows by now, and believe me, they don't need the extra ammunition."

"Oh, darling." Verna sighed. "Why don't you comply? Go in there, give her whatever DNA she wants, so you can end it, once and for all."

"I'm not giving her anything."

"What can it hurt?"

"I'll tell you what it can hurt. I know the baby isn't mine, but the second I give that woman a vial of my blood, I'll be admitting she might be right. And then I'll start wishing she would be because every baby should grow up with a dad. And before you know it, I'm there in the delivery room, cutting the cord of what was never mine to begin with."

"Nicki know?"

"How the hell do you raise a conversation like that? 'Welcome to south Florida, and by the way, my ex-girlfriend is pregnant, and she says it's mine.' Of course I haven't told her. It's ludicrous."

"She might understand, being's she grew up without a daddy."

"Yeah, I thought of that. But..." He shook his head. "Ironically, that's why I haven't told her yet. She'll want me to be the father, even if I know I'm not."

"Don't keep this secret. Nicki might be just the friend you need right about now."

He rubbed a hand over his face.

"Sooner rather than later, you tell her. Tonight, if you're thinking straight. Take her out. Somewheres romantic." Verna raised the bottle of beer to her lips and chugged a healthy swallow. "You can probably still get a late table at Casa Blanca."

He stared at the graphite on his hands. "I have a long day tomorrow, and she needs the sleep. Maybe tomorrow."

*   *   *

He crept into his bedroom with two of Nicki's three suitcases and quietly placed them on the floor. He turned his gaze to the bed, where twisted sheets hid her body from the waist down.

Her sleeping figure provided immeasurable inspiration—for more than the artist in him. He again imagined her in a dark studio, this time with a crisp, white sheet concealing all parts of her not meant for public viewing, back arched against an onyx table, one knee up, hands pressed at her sides, gripping for something to ground her as she gave into pure pleasure.

The near-wet dream halted. She didn't need a good sexing, no matter how good she looked in his bed. No matter that she stoked a raging fire in him. Right now, she needed someone to hold her, support her. He crawled into bed behind her and slipped an arm around her waist, his physical protection coming twenty-four hours too late.

She sank into his embrace, kicked his ankle, and breathed a wonderful sigh. He tightened his hold and closed his eyes.

CHAPTER 3

Ty awakened, Nicki's abandoned pillow warm in the crook of his arm. The clock read 5:42. Nearly quarter-to-five, her time. So early.

The sheets, when ruffled, emitted a waning scent of vanilla laced with raspberry. He sank back into his pillow, savored the feminine scent, and ached for the chance to hold her again. The innate yearning consumed him the way the tide engulfed the shore—a natural, uninhibited course of action he was powerless to deny.

But that didn't mean he had to act on it. So she'd awakened the long-dead artist within him. So he'd discovered her intimate, black-and-blue secret. Did it matter that he hadn't felt an attraction of this enormity in...well, ever? She was still Nicki, albeit fuller and curvier than he remembered, and he was still her protector.

He crawled from bed—*still dressed, good boy*—and pattered into the hallway. After peeking into the three torn-apart bedrooms and gutted bathroom without finding her, he walked down the stairs.

"Hey, bright eyes."

Midway to the kitchen, he turned toward her sweet voice, rubbed a thumb over an eye, and spotted her through the open front door. She was sitting on the porch and gazing into the rising sun. "Hey, kid."

Her hair was a riotous mess, and a black smudge of mascara smeared at the outside corner of her right eye. When she breathed in, she lifted her chin to the salmon sky. "Beautiful, isn't it?"

"Sure is." He'd never seen something as naturally pretty his entire life. And she was still wearing his sweatshirt.

She patted the vacant porch. "Come here."

"Can't sleep?"

"Can't miss this." She nodded toward the east to the sun creeping up over the rooftops. A morning breeze, carrying salt of the Atlantic on its wings, swept over the isle.

Whenever he filled his lungs with pure south Florida air, he felt a renewed sense of purpose, an unwavering source of encouragement. "I belong here." He sat next to her.

"I think you do." She leaned into him. "You even look local. So tan, and I dare say those streaks in your hair aren't courtesy of a stylist. You wear coats when it's seventy degrees outside, don't you?"

He placed his arm around her shoulders. "Yeah, it's funny what you get used to."

"It is, isn't it?" Her cheek met his shoulder, and she looked up at him.

He fought the urge to tuck a wild curl behind her ear and lost himself in her innocent gaze. "Why do you do it? Why do you pose?"

She licked her pale pink lips. "Why do you want to win the Key? Why do you want to win Custom Homebuilder of the Year?"

"I want to prove I'm capable."

"To whom? Your father?"

"No. Myself."

When she nodded, her hair rumpled against his chest.

"Why do you pose?" he asked.

"Why does it bother you so much?"

"You're naked up there. Why shouldn't it bother me?"

"It isn't political. It's just my body."

"You shouldn't use your body that way." But God, she was good at it. Disciplined posture, enticing from every angle. The curves of her figure, the arch in her back...perfect.

"Are you afraid I'll sleep with the students who draw me?"

"No, I'm afraid they'll want to sleep with you. I've been there, been one of them. Not every guy in that room will respect you."

"That's okay because—"

"No, it isn't."

"Yes it is. If I posed for you, would it change the way you felt about me? Would you automatically want to sleep with me, just because you drew me?"

No. I want to sleep with you for a thousand other reasons.

"I respect myself," she said. "I don't care if they think a girl like me

25

has lesser values than one who doesn't have what it takes to climb onto that pedestal. I know what I am, and I owe that to you."

"I don't want credit, not for that."

"But it's true. You helped me realize I can do anything I want."

"So now you know you're capable, stop."

She turned and zapped him with a dark, mysterious stare. "If you win the Key, are you going back to Chicago?"

"It's not the same thing."

"It's a different medium is all, but the result is the same. It's art, one way or another."

"Let's make a deal. Keep your clothes on while you're here, and I'll let you help behind the scenes, and show you how capable you are on a job site."

"What makes you think you can 'let me' do anything?"

"While you're staying with me, I'm responsible for you."

"Yes, Mother."

"Somehow I doubt those words ever passed through your mother's lips." He stroked the hair from her face. "But speaking of Jeanine, call her today. Let her know where you are before she starts to worry."

"My phone isn't ringing, is it?"

"Regardless, call her. And I can't have you on site during the work week for insurance reasons, but you can help on the weekends, on the sly. I can feed you, and, of course, you're welcome to stay as long as you want."

"All that for the pleasure of your company? Care to sweeten the deal with the keys to a certain convertible?"

He smiled and rubbed his knuckles across the crown of her head before brushing his lips into her hair. *Nothing like the smell of a woman in the morning.* "Not a chance."

The sound of an approaching vehicle captured his attention and he released her. "Get ready. We have to leave for the site in a few minutes." He nudged her toward the door.

A white SUV rumbled into view. *What's she doing here?* He glanced over his shoulder to see that Nicki was already out of sight. After a quick sigh of relief, he rushed to the foot of his driveway, leaned against the driver's open window, and greeted his unexpected visitor. "'Morning, Mandy."

"Hi." Despite the early hour, she was fully made up, not a chestnut strand of hair out of place. "You're up early."

He nodded. "Overtime. How are you feeling?"

"Stop pretending to care."

"I care."

Her black eyes turned to glass. "Why are you doing this, Ty? If you care so damn much—"

"I'm pretty good with calculations, and I paid attention every time I had you in my bed. If that baby were mine, I'd know it."

"Have you considered that maybe my doctor's wrong about the due date?"

No. He combed through his tangled hair with his fingers and looked to the sunrise. This conversation—if he had to have it, and apparently, he did—was better suited for later in the day, when he'd had a chance to put on a shirt and brush his teeth. "Why don't you pay Tabor a visit at the crack of dawn? God knows it wouldn't be the first time."

"Tell me you aren't fixating on that one time when—"

"A productive one time, if you ask me." He nodded at the four-and-a-half month swell of her abdomen and began to turn away.

"Nothing happened that morning, and you know it."

"You take care."

"This has nothing to do with the way I feel about you. It's about the baby. Our baby."

He took a step toward the house. "Take care."

"Ty?"

He stopped. "Yeah?"

"It's a girl."

An icy sensation shimmied through him, and he inhaled a lungful of air. "Congratulations." His first step was a difficult maneuver, but once he took it, he didn't look back.

The crunch of stones beneath tires indicated Mandy had driven away. At least he could thank his lucky stars she hadn't pursued him on foot, but her words followed, as if floating at his back. "It's a girl." Suddenly, the baby was more than a fetus. She was a she.

*   *   *

"I'll be damned." Ty parked Betty in front of the job site and drummed his fingers against the gearshift.

Nicki stopped rolling the cuffs of her jeans and snapped her eyes away from his fascinating, callused hands. "What?"

"We have company." He pulled the Wayfarers from the bridge of his nose and met her gaze. "Joe Montalvo. The journeyman framer you met yesterday." He scanned her from head to toe. "What's with all the skin? This is a construction site, not a nightclub."

"A ninety-degree construction site."

"And you shouldn't be wearing sandals."

"I heard you the first fifty times. Who packs boots for a trip to south Florida? I'll go shopping tomorrow."

"Step on a nail, and I'll deny I even know you." He turned off the car, reached into the back seat, and retrieved his tape measure. "You should wear a hardhat."

"No one's roofing. What's going to fall on me?"

"I might drop something down the stairwell."

"So, don't."

He fixed her with a hard stare and exited the car. "How is my crew supposed to listen to me, when you won't?"

"Fine." She climbed out of the car. "Where can I find one?"

"Thank you. In the trunk." He tossed a ring of keys to her. "And before you even consider it, I can hear the whine of this motor from worlds away."

She rolled her eyes. "Everything's about the car, isn't it? You want one?"

"One what?" He looked up from clipping his tape measure to his belt, a gleam in his eyes.

"A hardhat. God, you're cranky."

He tapped his fingers against his lean hips and sighed. "Sorry. And no. You're wearing mine." With that he kicked at a dry lump of dirt on the road and turned toward the house.

At first, his pace was slow and steady, thumb flicking at the tape measure. Halfway there, he quickened his steps, reached into his back pocket for his Three-peat hat, and stuffed it backwards onto his blond head.

Was there a dishwasher back at the chaos he called a home? She'd heard baseball caps washed well in dishwashers. It was worth a try anyway. Assuming, of course, she could pry it off his head.

She opened Betty's trunk to find a trove of discarded items: dusty golf clubs, a deflating basketball, a red handkerchief—maybe starched, maybe stiff with rigor mortis—screwdrivers, a trim hammer... No wonder he'd put her suitcases in the backseat yesterday. Nothing more would fit in the trunk, that's for sure. Good thing he didn't keep a job site the way he kept his personal property.

*   *   *

With sausage-like thumbs tucked into the pockets of his jeans, Montalvo leaned a broad shoulder against a second-story window and nodded toward street level. "So who's the chick? She gonna be here every day now?"

"No." Ty fought a deep sigh and squinted into the morning sun, already hot and beating down mercilessly on his shoulders. It seemed the journeyman had an ulterior motive for reporting to work, other than time-and-a-half pay. Well, if he could work and look at Nicki at the same time, so be it, as long as he kept his hands to himself. "She's just an old friend."

"She's sweet."

"So's your wife, I bet."

Montalvo turned away from what Ty knew was a stunning view, landscape aside. "Yep. And pregnant again."

Mentioning the wife had been a desperate attempt to change the subject, a guess, as the man didn't boast his marital status with a wedding ring. "Your second?"

"Fourth."

Fourth? Who knew? "Congratulations."

Montalvo again motioned toward Nicki. "So what's her story?"

"She's here to help us win the Key."

"Shit, Carmichael, we don't got a chance in hell of winning that Key. You think you can cruise in with your Armani ties and tasseled shoes and win a Key?" He snapped his fingers and shook his head. "Go try for a Key in your own neck of the woods. Bertolli's got this one in the bag."

"So he's gotten lucky a few years running. If he's never won Custom Homebuilder of the Year—and he hasn't, right?—he can't be that good."

"And you are? Seen the latest Bertolli concept house?"

Ty nodded. "He's got an almighty dollar behind it, but we've got something he lost long ago—ambition."

"And we got her, too, huh?" Montalvo cracked a smile and leered at Nicki. "She any good?"

Ty forced himself to ignore the sexual inference and swallowed the urge to set the journeyman straight. "She's brilliant. Just doesn't know it yet."

Montalvo crossed his arms in front of his chest. "Is she going to change any dimensions up here, or should we get started?" When he turned back to Ty, he looked him square in the eye.

Ty held the gaze until the carpenter looked away. "Let's start in bedroom five," Ty said.

"You're in charge here." Montalvo shuffled behind. "But I bet she's in charge in the bedroom."

Ty tightened his fists, and without a break in stride said, "She's here for one reason."

"Same reason you kept Mandy around?"

He spun to face him. "Let's get one thing straight."

"You want to throw down?" Montalvo chuckled. "Didn't think you had it in you."

"We're here to work. If you want to gossip, find a sewing circle." He refused to blink until Montalvo nodded.

In silence, the two men walked to the space above the garage and began erecting the frame of a wall.

"Hello?" Nicki's voice floated up from the ground level.

"Where've you been?" Ty wiped sweat from his forehead with the back of his sawdust-covered hand and meandered toward the two-story foyer. He leaned against a stud and watched through the stairwell as Nicki sauntered into the house. Flared jeans cuffed to mid-calf, T-shirt tied above her midriff, and carefully tended toes peeking out of beach sandals. She looked no more at home in a rough-framed residence than she would riding on a garbage truck. At least she'd listened regarding the hardhat.

She tapped her toes twice against the first floor deck and perched her dainty hands on her hips above a... *Hey, she found my favorite tool belt.*

"You think it's easy finding something in that mess of a trunk?" She looked up at him and tucked a curl under the scuffed, white rim of the too-large hat.

"I never seem to have trouble."

"Well, now I won't either." She licked her lips. "Where do you want me?"

I don't know, but I can tell you where I want that mouth. "Come on up. Say hi to Montalvo."

She traversed up the stairs without tremor, fiddling with the buckle of the tool belt. Obviously, the less-than-sturdy stairs and open air of the second floor didn't scare her. Although she didn't look like she belonged on site, she carried herself as if she balanced stories above the ground and wove around two-by-fours daily.

And that rear end...such definition. He could watch her climb stairs for centuries.

"Hello." She extended her hand to Montalvo. "We nearly met yesterday. Nicolette Paige."

The framer's jaw descended a fraction of an inch, and he ogled her with a quick head-to-toe glance. He wiped his hand against his shirt and grasped her hand. "Ma'am."

"Let's get started," she said.

*   *   *

By midday, the sun scorched overhead. The damn hardhat, a sweaty nuisance, slipped into Nicki's eyes whenever she crouched to pencil a mark for cutting. But she willed herself to keep it planted atop her head, in an attempt to follow Ty's orders. If she respected Ty's authority on the jobsite, perhaps Montalvo would, too.

If Ty earned this journeyman's respect, chances were the rest of the crew would follow suit. Montalvo was more than a carpenter; he was a craftsman with speed and accuracy. They'd framed the two bedrooms above the garage and the shared bath between before noon.

When Montalvo ran for lunch, she afforded herself the luxury of discarding the hat. The balmy, Atlantic breeze swept across the back of her neck, a refreshing breath against her moist skin, and the shade of the lower level was an oasis in the hot sun.

Ty removed his shirt on the far side of the structure and slipped it through his belt loop. With the sun shining in off the ocean, he was a muscled silhouette in a rough doorway. He was too far away to hear her heavy sigh, but the sight of him sent shivers up her spine. *So that's what swinging a hammer everyday will do to a man. Wow.*

He turned toward her. "Are you holding up all right?"

She nodded and took a swig from her water bottle. "You need forty-five inches for that tub deck upstairs. Forty-eight would better."

"What'd I frame?"

"Forty-two."

With a hitched hip and a dusty hand traveling across his chin, he chewed his lip for a moment. "It's a thirty-six inch soaker. We're fine."

"Sure, there's room for the lip of the tub and a backsplash. But where the hell are you going to mount a faucet?"

He kicked at the floor and turned away, only to zap her with an electric stare over his shoulder. "Why didn't you say anything up there?"

"And discount you in front of Montalvo ? Are you kidding?" She

31

licked salty sweat from her upper lip. "I'm surprised one of you didn't catch it. You're working too fast, Ty. You're going to make mistakes."

"When no one's looking, I'll yank it back up and move it out six inches. Thanks."

"Don't thank me. Tell me I don't have to wear this damn hat anymore."

"But in the future, let me know. Don't let me waste time building it wrong." His half smile crept into view as he approached and sat beside her. "You're handling him well, you know."

"Who, Montalvo?" She waved his words away and took another sip of water. "Child's play. He may talk a good game behind my back, but there's nothing there. Too in love with his wife, right?"

"How'd you know he was married?"

She shrugged. "Something in the way he talks to me."

"He isn't talking, he's leering. You might think about untying that shirt and hiding your skin a little more."

"First, if he's the one 'leering,' which he isn't, by the way, why am I getting the lecture? Second, married men don't 'leer.' They search for something wrong when they look at a woman, for a reason to stay true to their vows. Single guys don't do that."

"How do you know anything about married men?" He nudged her with his elbow, and if not for the perspiration pouring down her back, she might have rested her tired body against him.

"I don't know a thing about men." The bruises on her back proved it. Hopefully, he'd take her word for it and drop the subject. "I assure you."

"All right. You don't have to wear the hat anymore." He brushed a finger over her cheek, and under his touch, she imagined undressing for him, posing at sunset while he concentrated on her body, recreated it on paper. Heaven on earth.

His thumb worked its way up her cheekbone, massaging with deep, intent strokes, and she looked up at him, the images of an artist and his subject fleeting through her mind. Was he thinking about drawing her, too?

"You're dirty," he said with a smile.

CHAPTER 4

A seductive sigh awakened Ty from an after-work doze in the dim light of his bedroom. Asleep on the next pillow, Nicki rolled toward him and closed the already small gap between them. Her knee met his upper thigh in a piercing stab, and she'd missed his jewels by only half an inch. After a partial recovery, an elbow flew at his chin, and he caught it.

"Damn it, Nicki." With a strong arm across her shoulders and a long leg across her hips, he braced her against the mattress.

Her breasts rose against him with even inhalations—a cruel temptation. He took a deep breath and stared at her mouth. So pink, like cotton candy. And only an inch away. What would it feel like to kiss a mouth like that?

Her lips parted with another incredible sigh, and he imagined the tip of her tongue teasing his lips, a soft hand meeting his cheek.

He relaxed against her body for a moment, aware of the cotton shorts resting low on her hips, conscious of a small patch of satin panties peeking out from beneath them and caressing his thigh.

Her breasts seemed to burn through her T-shirt, and he began to harden. The contour of her body against his chest lured him to the boundary between self-control and animal instinct. With every ounce of determination, he battled the urge to push her shirt aside and cup her breasts in his hands.

"Mmmm."

If she didn't stop making that noise…

His heart sashayed, and visions of bruises sparked in his mind. Someone else had recently lost control with her body. He collapsed to his pillow, and ignored the innate yearning to pull off her clothing and bury his erection into the warm—and he knew for certain she was warm—moist valley between her legs.

*   *   *

She opened her eyes, caught her breath, and stared at him.

He licked his lips as he stared back. "Hi."

The obscure recollection of a kiss and an indescribable closeness tantalized her. The look in his eyes confirmed it—a tinge of regret, along with overwhelming heat. "What happened?"

"I'm defending myself. You're dangerous."

It wasn't until he raised a hand from her shoulder that she realized he'd imprisoned her against the mattress. Something long and hard pressed against her hip when he lifted his leg from across hers. *Oh my, that's his—*

"You must be hungry," he said.

Well, that was one way to put it. "What time is it?"

"Ten to nine."

"A.M. or P.M.?"

His half-smile appeared. "P.M."

"Were you...I'm sorry if this is inappropriate, but I could've sworn...did you kiss me?"

He shook his head, even as his tongue roved over his bottom lip.

"Really?" Her lips tingled, as if recently massaged.

"I'd remember, don't you think?"

But her breasts sizzled with unfulfilled desire, and she felt an aroused sensation in her clit. If memory served, that's what sex felt like just before it happened.

Her cheeks flushed with heat, and for a moment, she wanted to maneuver around him, to position his hard parts where her soft parts wanted them to be.

He rolled away. "Are you hungry? I don't have much downstairs, but I think I have a box of chocolates stashed in Betty's glove compartment." His smile flashed again.

"Starving, actually."

"Well, you worked hard today, and you've barely eaten since you got here. Veggie sub for lunch. What's up with that?" He rose from the bed, adjusted his sweat shorts, and stretched toward the ceiling.

"There's a great steak place on the beach. We can eat outside."

Her eyes glazed over as she watched his muscled body move. She'd give anything to feel those arms flexing around her, those hips grinding against hers. And thirty seconds ago, she'd nearly made it happen.

"Don't tell me you're a vegetarian now," he said. "But even if you are, these steaks are reason enough to change your beliefs."

She blinked into his gaze. "No. Meat's fine." She sounded nonchalant, but her heart raced with a ravenous pulse. She was famished, for more than dinner.

"Tell you what. I'll give you some space, get you a drink or something, and when you're ready, we'll fly." He headed toward the hallway. "Water? Wine?" He clamped his hand against the white door trim.

"Whatever you're having."

"I'm having a beer."

"Fine."

"You don't drink beer."

"I can."

"That's what you want? Are you sure?"

"Yes."

With her nod, he walked away.

She peered around the corner and studied his square shoulders, which had broadened since he'd left Chicago. His new profession hadn't seemed to suit him when he'd first told her about it, but it certainly looked good on him now.

He felt good, too. That sinewy arm holding her in place, that strong leg. And he'd been *hard.* Ready. Had she inspired his arousal, or had he simply awakened that way? She crawled out of bed and made her way to the bathroom, splashed water on her face, and met her eyes in the mirror.

The cold water did little to chase away the feeling of Ty's strong body against hers. She wasn't sure she wanted the feeling to wane, but she couldn't surrender to it either. For years, she'd fantasized about turning him on, but the prospect of losing his friendship had held her in check. Rock. Hard place. *And he'd been rock hard, all right.*

They couldn't jeopardize sixteen years of camaraderie, no matter how good they might be together. Fort Lauderdale—and Ty Carmichael—were part of a dreamland, where everything felt right, and at this juncture, she needed to feel respectable. She lifted her T-shirt and turned her back toward the mirror. Besides, he'd go insane with revenge if he ever saw her bruises.

When she finished primping, she returned to the bedroom to dress. Ty entered simultaneously, placed a bottle of beer atop the dusty dresser, and brought another to his lips. "That was fast," he said.

"This room borders dangerously on art deco, bright eyes." She fingered through the clothing she'd worn the day before, carefully folded and positioned on the nightstand.

"What do you have against art deco anyway?" He started toward the closet.

"It's the folly of the interior design industry." She lifted the rumpled comforter and peered between the sheets. "When I was working with your dad, no sooner would I finish a deco job than it was out-of-date."

"I'll keep you out of Miami then. Half that city's art deco."

"Thanks for the warning."

"What are you looking for?"

"I'm missing a bra. The white one. From yesterday."

"Yeah, I saw it. Very nice."

She rolled her eyes. "Thanks."

"What are you wearing tonight?"

"Something basic and black, if that's all right with you."

He shrugged. "Fine. I fail to see why you need a white bra, if you're wearing black, that's all."

"Some people like to know where their things are." She dropped to the floor and peered under the bed.

"Don't go under there, Nicki. You might not find your way out."

"How do you live like this? Nothing's where it belongs."

"Because it doesn't belong anywhere."

"Exactly. How do you find anything?"

"What'd you lose?"

"Am I having this conversation by myself? My white bra."

"Lacey? Demi-cup?"

She popped up from the floor to find him sporting a teasing smile at the closet door, the beer bottle dangling from his hand.

"Like I said"—his grin widened—"very nice."

"Where is it?"

"It's in here." He entered the closet, placed his beer high on a shelf, and closed the door a few inches. "I tripped on it, so I picked it up."

"Should I write the date down?" She stepped toward the closet and pushed the door open. "It's a red-letter day that you pick something—"

She gasped and covered her smile as Ty yanked boxer shorts up and over his nude bottom. "I'm sorry. I didn't realize you were—"

"It's on the hook behind you."

"Sorry." She grabbed the bra, ducked out of the closet without obsessing over the untidiness of his wardrobe, and reached for her beer.

"You think I should wear a tie?" he asked, peeking out at her as he stepped into a pair of khaki-colored pants.

She met his gaze, but quickly looked away, embarrassed she had seen his nude bottom. Her cheeks were probably plunging to deep crimson, and beer dribbled down her chin in her distraction.

"I have tons of ties," he said. "Don't really have many chances to wear them anymore, though."

"If you want to wear one, wear one." The image of his bare backside, nothing but white muscle amid the rest of his tanned flesh, was branded into her mind. She might never forget the look of it. Perhaps another gulp of beer might cause a lapse of amnesia.

"Hey, Nicki."

Just as she turned toward his voice, a balled-up black-and-olive casual tie hit her in the chest.

"How's that one? Still in style?" He rolled his sleeves to his forearms as he approached her. He had yet to button the shirt, and his scrumptious pecs and abs were more than visible.

She took a deep breath and pretended to study the tie. "It's fine."

"But?"

"But I think the shirt makes enough of a statement on its own."

*   *   *

The porch lamps cast streams of light across her curves in all the right places, capturing the bounce of her breasts as she bounded off the front steps. "Can I drive?"

Was she wearing a bra? He glanced at her and saw no sign of one— no lines across the breasts where cup met flesh, no peeking straps. Either she was braless or it was a really great piece of lingerie.

"I'll take that as a yes." She wiggled her fingers.

"You're kidding, right? You don't know where we're going."

"I take direction very well."

He locked his gaze on her. The sleeveless, black dress clung to her hourglass figure as if it were made to showcase those breasts, those hips. She tapped her open-toed sandals against the stones on the driveway.

"I'm sure you do." He envisioned her sprawled atop the bed she'd insisted on making before they left asking him what he wanted her to do, satisfying his every animal need. He imagined his hands wandering from her pink toenails to the secrets hidden between her thighs.

"I'll clean your bathtub." She stepped closer.

"You'll probably clean it anyway." There was something alluring about the scent of her. Maybe she had spritzed her hair with perfume, a clean, floral fragrance that blended with the raspberry-vanilla scent of her skin. Whatever it was, it drove him into a frenzy. He blinked down into her eyes. "A grungy tub's never bothered me, but it'll drive you insane if you have to step into that grime one more time. I'm shocked you managed to shower in there at all. Try again."

"Let's go at it from a different angle."

Yes, let's go at it.

Her lips pressed into a half pucker. "Tell me what it'll take."

I was just going to ask you the same question. What will it take to get me kissing your toes, licking you behind your knees? Let's see where it takes us. Let's follow, wherever it leads. His eyes began to close as he imagined doing naughty things to her. He wanted to inhale between her breasts, place tiny, wet kisses around her nipples, which were probably rosy, round, and perfect. He wanted to stick his tongue into her navel—and into something else, too—and tease her with playful bites down to her hips.

He snapped open his eyes and pulled the keys away in the split second before she snatched them. "Maybe some other time, all right?"

She pulled off her shoes and climbed into Betty without opening the door. Her dressed hiked up, but she did not pull it down, even when she sank into the seat next to seven pink roses. She set the bouquet upon the dash without giving it a second thought and propped her bare feet next to it. Her short dress crept high up her thighs, exposing a smidgen of her panties for anyone who dared to crane his neck. What a divine view.

"Nice panties."

"Pardon me?"

Did he say that aloud? He cleared his throat and slid behind the wheel. "We have reservations, but we still might have to wait. They're pretty busy this time of night."

"That's all right."

"To tide you over—" He reached under her legs and opened the glove box, his hand grazing against the underside of her bare thighs.

"—I know you like chocolate cherries."

She laughed. "I thought you were kidding."

He tossed the box of candy into her lap. "Girls like chocolate, right? And watch those thorns." He nodded at the roses.

"Those are for me?"

"They're from Verna's garden, and I don't wade through that mess for Betty."

"Betty, two thousand; Nicki, one."

"Take it as an apology. I'm sorry I didn't meet you at the airport." *And I'm sorry I wasn't there to stop whatever happened to you in Chicago.*

"Forgiven." She popped a cherry into her mouth as he drove east toward the ocean.

A few minutes later, he turned onto A1A and parked the car near the promenade edged with Fort Lauderdale's signature white wave wall. He took her hand and escorted her out of the car. "We're a ways away, but it's a nice night for a stroll down the broadwalk, if you can avoid the skaters."

"Broadwalk? Not boardwalk?"

"Right. It's a Lauderdale thing, but just a fancy name for the sidewalk along the beach."

She raised her eyes to look at the stars, and he wondered again about the marks on her body. Maybe he should ask about them, demand answers. Then again, he had a little explaining—about a baby girl—to do, himself.

To his left, across A1A, patrons scurried in and out of shops and restaurants, their banter a friendly murmur, compared to what he had to confess to Nicki. On his right, fiber-optic lights blended from blues to purples along the wave wall, its scallops reminiscent of rudimentary waves. If only life were as simple as a child's vision of the ocean.

He gazed beyond the white, sculpted waves, entranced by those riding in with the Atlantic tide. Torn between his need to come clean and his desire to bury Mandy's paternity suit, he breathed in the salty ocean air and offered her his hand. "A nice night for a walk, and a nice night for a chat."

"A chat?" She laced her fingers into his. "Are you going to tell me about your secretary?"

His stomach knotted. "How do you know about her?"

"Montalvo mentioned something."

"What'd he say?"

"Not much."

"Well, there's not much to tell."

"Just a quick roll in the hay turned bitter?"

Not exactly. "Something like that," he said. "Now tell me what happened with this guy in Chicago who you're running from."

She shrugged and looked away. "What do you want to know?"

"Just what he did to you."

"I don't think that's necessary."

He tightened his grip on her hand, stopped walking, and pulled her closer. The perfume in her hair wafted around him, sent a shiver like a bolt of lightning down his spine and settled between his legs. "Nicki Jeanne."

At last, she looked up at him.

"He's not what you deserve, is he?" He brushed the indentation in her chin with his thumb. "Far from it, judging by what I've seen."

She began to shake her head. "What have you seen to—"

"Bruises. I was drawing you, and I saw—"

"You were drawing me?" She frowned. "When?"

"Yesterday, while you were sleeping."

"Why did you do that?"

"You invited me to, if you remember."

"And you actually did it?" Her eyes began to glow with anger. "While I was sleeping?"

"Relax, Nicki. I didn't undress you or anything."

"I didn't think you undressed—"

"Anyway, it was just a tiny part of you."

"What part?"

"This one." He gently placed a hand onto her back and pulled her closer still.

Her gaze fluttered up to meet his, and her lips parted. "Ty."

She pressed her hands against his racing heart, and instantly, he warmed from his core to his fingertips and toes. He wanted to nip those pretty pink lips and feel her tongue against his.

With her right index finger, she traced a button hole, maneuvered her way into it, and tickled his bare skin with the tip of her finger. "Why did you draw me?"

"I had to," he whispered.

She lowered her head, as if she were studying the patterns her finger drew on his chest. "That's not fair." Without warning, she turned away, leaving his arms aching to hold her again as she walked further down the broadwalk.

"You told me to draw you." His words chased after her.

Heads of passing couples turned to gauge her reaction to his declaration. Ty waited, hands in pockets. She couldn't go far. But she refused to turn around.

"I'm sorry I offended you," he said.

Near an oversized, cylindrical newel post, *Las Olas* lettered in black capitals on it, she stopped with an abrupt click of her heel against the red and black bricks. For a moment, he didn't know if she would race into the sand and plunge into the ocean, or if she'd turn and face him.

The calming hush of the waves hitting the shore filled his ears. She must have noticed their lulling sound, too, because she turned and looked out over the white sand beach, gazing at the midnight-blue beyond.

"This is exactly what I mean by a double standard." She turned her gaze to his, her voice as mesmerizing as the surf. "You don't agree with what I do. You think posing cheapens my body. You think it gives men the wrong idea about me, but it's fine when you've got a pencil in your hand."

Damn right, it's fine.

She fingered a curl and looked back to the beach. "You need to get over this obsession with protecting me from every little thing. This world isn't a bubble, Ty. Bad things are going to happen, and yes, they're going to happen to me."

"What happened?"

"What happened isn't the point."

"Right. The point is you invited me to draw you. So I did."

"You should've waited for an appropriate time."

"I don't know that there was a more perfect moment to change my point of view, Nicki."

"To change your point of view?" She glared at him, a sharp contrast to the seductive tone flowing like a symphony from her vocal chords. The lights flickered to bright pink along the wave wall and illuminated her shapely figure. "Do you feel different now?"

"Well, yeah." He began to walk toward her. "But not in the way you probably think."

"Elaborate." She tapped her toes twice against the bricks, her posture far too rigid to relax against the wave wall, although he wished she would.

He pictured her nude body settled in the swale of a wave, resting her back against its swell, arms stretched above her head. Chin pointed toward the sun, tiny tummy begging to be kissed as he drew her from a random location on the promenade.

"I don't want to elaborate," he said.

"You see why this is unfair? I wasn't part of it. Something changed in you, between us, because of my body, and you didn't extend me the courtesy of sharing it."

He walked closer. "I guess I can understand that."

"Wake me next time."

"Next time? What makes you think I'm going to do it again, after that response?"

"Oh, we're doing it again. The right way…when we're both awake. After dinner. Just as soon as I drive that car."

"I don't know. I'm not very good anymore. I haven't done anything like that in a long time, and I don't think I want to do it again so soon."

"Why not?"

"It's exhausting. It's dire concentration, it's hand cramps. It's—"

"What if I say you don't have a choice?"

Then I'll have to admit I can't look at you without wanting you. Concentrating on your nude body will inevitably lead to doing something we can't undo. We'll risk everything, and considering Mandy's condition, I've sacrificed my quota for the sake of sex this year. "I do have a choice, Nicki." He forced a smile. "It's my car."

"Not everything is about that damn car." She pivoted and continued to walk along the broadwalk.

*   *   *

"I'm sorry," he said.

The comfort of his hand molding around hers sent a ripple of contentment through her, and she rested her head on his shoulder. They walked down A1A to a charming old house on Alhambra Street, situated on a patch of land with views of both the Atlantic Ocean and the intracoastal waterway.

The Casablanca Café's herringbone brick patio, lined with pewter lanterns, boasted a handful of round, green granite tables. A single champagne flute centered on each table held a nosegay of a dozen pink and white rosebuds and baby's breath.

A dusting of smooth sand, brushed in from the beach, settled in the crevices between the bricks. She looked toward the water now, the wave wall lights fading from yellow to green.

Palms rustled in the night breeze, keeping time with the splash of the waves, and the moonlight cast myriads of twinkling diamonds into the surf from shore to horizon. If this wasn't Eden, paradise didn't exist.

The aroma of Mediterranean spices lured her attention to the amber stucco of the historical house, and she followed it—and the pull of Ty's hand—inside.

Beneath what appeared to be a mahogany beamed ceiling, he nudged his way to the bar, her hand still nestled in his. "What do you want?" He turned sideways against the bar and guided her close.

She slid into a narrow slot between him and another patron's back. Only inches separated them, and if she breathed too deeply, her breasts would surely touch his chest. "I'll have a cabernet."

"Good choice." He turned toward the bartender, and brushed against her body. "Bottle of the Kenwood Cab. '99 or 2000, if you have it."

He looked down at her with a half-smile. "What?"

"Nothing. We're awfully close, that's all."

"Close quarters, kid."

She breathed deeply, and her breasts heaved against him, just as she knew they would. They were close, all right. Close in proximity, and close to doing things they probably shouldn't do. Terrifying and thrilling.

They'd held hands before, in Chicago, but in a more playful, flirty manner. Usually he did it when he'd wanted to thwart the attention of another woman, but never for such a long stretch of time. And he had never touched her in the intimate, familiar ways reserved for lovers before, either, brushing her chin, raking through her hair. There were the roses. He'd given her candy.

And he'd drawn her. Not all of her, granted, but a tiny, insignificant part of her that suddenly seemed private. She wondered why he had chosen to draw her back, and what he might want to draw later.

And that's the way he was looking at her, too—as if he couldn't decide what he wanted to see next. Her heart fluttered. "What's going on, Ty?"

"With what?"

"This." She lifted their interlaced hands to his chest. "You. Me."

His eyes darkened and his intense stare settled upon her.

*　　　*　　　*

She was looking up at him in the most quizzical of ways. Pleading. Accusing. Wanting.

And through his thin shirt, he felt her nipples tickling up and down against his chest with every breath. Her lips shone with a pink-tinted gloss he wanted to kiss away, and her lashes seemed miles long and thick, and either he'd been staring at her for an eternity, or she'd blinked a hundred times in the past few seconds.

"I'm responsible for you," he managed to say. "Just like always."

"It's different here."

"It's a different world here in south Florida. Lots of things are different."

The bartender poured two glasses of wine and left the bottle in exchange for a few twenties.

"I don't use credit cards anymore," Ty backed away from her. "It's harder to keep on top of them once hurricane season hits. Paychecks are random sometimes."

"Don't change the subject."

He fixed his gaze on the multitudes of bottles behind the bar for long moments, and tightened his grip on her hand. "Heads turn when you walk into a room, you know that?" At last, he looked at her.

She was shaking her head. "They're not looking at me."

"Yes, they are." He placed a wineglass within her reach. "Try it."

Her brow knit and her lips parted, as if she were about to rebut.

"Just drink it," he said with a sigh.

She brought the glass to her lips.

"People have always looked at you, Nicki." He stared at the top of the bar, twisting his glass against the dark green granite. "Even ten years ago, when you were too lanky and skinny. And more so since you've filled out. You have a way about you, there's something wise in the way you look at me, and even at your worst, your energy is amazing. You've got it all together."

"No, I—"

"Yes, you do. You have a mother who can't give you the time of day, a father you've never met—and believe me, if I ever find him, I'll give him a piece of my mind—yet still, you carry yourself in such a way…" *There's that wisdom again, in those seductive eyes.* "You're every guy's dream, as far I see it. So if you're asking if I'm attracted to that dream, if I'm attracted to you, the answer is obvious." He sipped again, or rather gulped, and when he returned his glass to the bar, he felt her looking at him.

Too nervous to look her in the eye after his confession, he waited for her to say something, but the something never came. Hesitantly, he glanced at her.

She was neither pleased nor angry. Worried, perhaps. Confused, definitely.

"That said, I know it'll never happen for us." He swirled the wine in his glass, while his heart pounded in a wild, uncontrolled beat. "There's no Ty-and-Nicki card out there. I won't sacrifice the trust you have in me, the trust I have in you, for a roll under the covers, however phenomenal it would be. Though I'm loath to admit it, you're safe with me."

She did not smile in relief, but she didn't cry either. Her lower lip started to stick out, but she quickly drew it back before it became a pout. She took a deep breath, and her breasts grazed up his chest in taunting persuasion. "I'm glad we agree on that."

*   *   *

Nicki propped a bare foot in his lap at their dinner table on the patio. He brushed white sand from her toes, wrapped a hand around her arch, and held her gaze.

The vague sense of wisdom appeared in her eyes again, and when she touched a flyaway curl at her left temple, he noticed a bruise on her wrist.

"Do you ever miss Chicago?" she asked.

He rubbed her foot from heel to toes. "Certain things about Chicago, yes."

"Like what?"

"Orange and yellow leaves on trees. Christmas on State Street." He squeezed her foot. "You."

"I've missed you, too."

"I'm sorry about the way I left without telling you."

"It's all right."

"Is it?" He looked again at the bruise on her left wrist. *All evidence is to the contrary.*

"It's going to be."

"Okay." He stared at her. Her tongue was tinged burgundy from the wine, and her cheeks glowed pink in the cool evening breeze. She was probably cold—her foot was—but if she was uncomfortable, her stoic posture denied it. She sat without a shiver or fidget.

"What was it like to leave everything you knew behind and take a flying leap of faith?"

He shrugged. "I don't know. I was too busy running to think about it at the time."

"Do you miss your parents? Your sisters?"

"The twins have enough going on in their own lives. They don't need me. Krissy's spending the year in France. Did you know that?"

"Yeah."

"And Freddi's still working with my father." Half a chuckle escaped him. "My father." He felt oddly detached from the man who had taught him everything about construction. Funny how he could use that knowledge every day without thinking of the man himself. He took a healthy sip of wine. "How is he?"

"How long has it been since you've spoken to him?"

"Let's see. How long have I been in Florida? In three months, it'll be two years. So I guess it would be about twenty-one months."

"I feel badly about that."

"It isn't your fault, Nicki Jeanne."

"Yes, it is. If you hadn't gone to bat for me, you'd still be there, in your father's good graces."

"There's more involved than my defending you over my sister's mistake. My father and I haven't agreed on anything since I was sixteen. And besides, I'm happier without him."

"He's always been hard on you," Nicki said.

Ty nodded. "Eat."

"I am eating."

"I'm going to fix that tub deck tomorrow."

"Need some help?"

"No, it won't take long. I'd do it Monday, but I'd rather not call it to the crew's attention."

"That's fine. It'll give me some time to clean the jungle you live in."

So calm, assured. What a change of pace, considering her recent middle-of-the-night phone call. "You were hysterical when you called that night."

She nodded. "I guess I was."

He stared at her, watched as she raised a tiny square of steak to her mouth. She wasn't going to say a word. "Did he rape you, Nicki?"

A stunned blink answered him.

"Nicki, talk to me."

"Why do you think he—"

"It looks like rough sex. I'm imagining the worse case scenario."

"Do you think I sleep with the students who draw me?"

He heard the clambering of his own heartbeat in his ears. *Bum, bum. Bum, bum.* "Was it a student? Did a student assume—"

"No." She trailed her fingers up and down the stem of her wineglass. "Most of them understand what I do. I'm asking if you do."

"I think I'm starting to."

"But you saw your models differently."

"Sure, I did. I wasn't serious about what I was doing."

"You were always amazing with a pencil in your hand."

"Having talent doesn't mean I had a passion for it. I cared more about getting laid than respecting the naked girls in the studio."

She sipped her wine, never losing eye contact with him. "Do you feel passionate about what you do now?"

"I think I've always wanted to work with my hands. But it was something my father wouldn't, and doesn't, understand. It's too blue-collar for his blood. Building is for those with GEDs, not me. I have a Master's degree, for God's sake."

"And yet you do it anyway."

"Nothing is about pleasing my father any more. I do what I love, and if my father can't accept that, let alone appreciate it, he cares more about himself than he does about me."

"That's how I feel about posing."

He wrapped a hand around her foot again, but only for the moment it took her to smile. "Listen, I can taste this Key Award. And you're going to help me, so no posing. You won't have time for it."

"What am I going to do all week while you're on site?"

"Once this house is framed, I'm on double duty. I'll be framing the Sykes project in Palm Beach, and overseeing the spec here in town. You'll have plenty to do at home. Make notes on layout, select colors, shop for window treatments and furniture for the open house."

"That can't be until September, the earliest. What am I going to do until—"

"Maybe nothing, but not posing." He leaned toward her, took her left hand in his, and brushed his thumb across her bare fourth finger. "I don't care if you spend your days sitting by the ocean, just looking pretty."

With a hint of a smile, she looked down at her plate. "Hardly, Ty."

"Every man on this beach has his eyes on you. I haven't felt this envied in a long time."

*   *   *

His blue eyes reflected the light of the lanterns surrounding the patio. One corner of his mouth peaked. An unruly, sun-kissed strand of hair slipped from atop his head. Amid the bustle of the restaurant, he seemed to blink in slow motion.

Her hand felt warm and safe in his, and she pulled her foot from his lap. No matter what he'd said earlier at the bar, he wasn't looking at her as if he were in control of his intentions. His gaze dripped with desire. He licked his lips and touched her on the chin, simultaneously squeezing her hand.

She leaned toward him and pressed a kiss onto his cheek.

He wove his fingers into her hair, and held her cheek-to-cheek. "You're a special woman," he whispered into her ear. With his thumb, he rubbed against the bruise on her wrist. "Heaven help the man who thought you weren't."

She closed her eyes and made a memory of the moment. *Grilled steak. Mediterranean spices. Salty, ocean air. A teasing of musky cologne.* "Thank you," she whispered.

He brushed a kiss near her ear.

A shiver darted through her, and an insatiable wanting tingled between her thighs. *He's drawing me tonight.*

CHAPTER 5

"Where do you want me?" Nicki wandered down Ty's hallway in bare feet. In her right hand, she held seven wilted pink roses, and in her left, she dangled her high-heeled sandals.

He watched her rear end wiggle with her gait.

"Are you listening to me?" She stopped walking and turned in his direction.

"Sure. I haven't thought about it." *In my bed, in the shower, on the porch, on the docks...just about anywhere. I'm not particular about where I make love to a woman.*

"Upstairs? Downstairs? I'm holding you to that rain check, by the way. I'll be driving that hunk of junk before I leave this state."

"We'll see."

A victorious smile touched her lips, and she dragged her right toe against her left ankle, as if scratching a mild itch. Such an ordinary motion, but he couldn't help wishing she were brushing something soft against him.

"Come here. This half of the house is closer to done." He pulled her by the hand toward the room Verna called the conservatory. Floor to ceiling windows provided a stunning moonlit setting, and situated in the center of the chipped limestone floor was Verna's snagged and faded chaise longue, upholstered in worn pink velvet.

Months ago, when he'd painted the room "Summer Song," the color of the Everglades, he'd pulled the single piece of furniture away from the wall, and the chaise never found its way back. Now he knew why:

49

destiny wanted Nicki's nude body displayed on that chaise, he was certain. "How's this?"

"Pretty." She handed her shoes to him and took a step toward the furniture. "And pink. Interesting choice for a bachelor."

"It was Verna's." He dropped her shoes. "I'll find a blanket, so you won't be cold."

"Occupational hazard. Besides, it's warm in Florida." She held up her hair, exposing a zipper at her back. "Help me out?"

He rubbed his suddenly sweaty hands together and brushed them against his pants. With a slight tremor, he raised his drawing hand to the zipper. "We don't have to do this, you know."

"I want to." Over her shoulder, she looked into his eyes. "Are you nervous?"

He began to shake his head, but then said, "Yeah. A little. Are you?"

"Always, in a new studio." Funny, she didn't shift in discomfort or even blink. "It's a matter of finding a comfort zone."

He inched the zipper down her back. "I know there are a lot of windows, but this room faces the garden. It's more private than it looks." *Will you look at that? No bra.*

He slipped his hands into the dress, against her bare, bruised back. Her skin was satiny soft, the marring invisible to the touch. If he hadn't seen the bruises with his own eyes, he never would have known they were there. "I don't want to hurt you."

She again spoke over her shoulder. "You won't."

He caressed his way to the spaghetti straps, lifted them over her shoulders. Along with the roses, the dress fell in a pool of black rayon at her feet, and he steadied her under the elbow as she stepped out of it.

He lowered his glance to her bottom. Situated below the nasty bruise, he found a black cotton, v-string thong. "Monogram series." He tucked his thumbs into the waistband.

She placed her hands atop his and firmly held them. *Right. She's capable of undressing herself.* "Sorry."

Illuminated in moonlight, she walked toward the chaise. At that moment, he gauged her reflection in the window across the room. Pert breasts, perfectly round. Tiny waist, balanced by her generous hips.

He turned away. "I'm going to get you a blanket."

"Ty."

"Yeah?" He stopped in his tracks, but didn't look back.

"Just get your paper and charcoal. I'm fine."

The springs of the chaise creaked. What position would he find her in when he returned? He hoped she would lie on her stomach. That way, he'd catch only a glimpse of her breasts. Maybe she'd go easy on him and keep her panties on, too. The fewer temptations, the better.

The walk to his bedroom seemed a mile long. When he finally reached his door, he adjusted his fly. Adjusted again. And again.

Frustrated with his own arousal, and the fact he could do nothing about it, he removed his khakis and stepped into a pair of plaid flannel pajama pants. More breathing room.

You had to tell her she was safe. Now you're stuck. Too turned on to finish yourself off, too bound to your promise not to touch her.

He'd certainly put himself in a difficult position. His promise had seemed a valiant idea at the time, but it was impractical. How could any man not touch a woman like this?

He shrugged out of his dinner shirt and traded it for a Diamond Custom Homes T-shirt, torn under the right arm. He opened his drawer for his small sketchpad, but changed his mind and rummaged under the bed for a pad twice as large. *If you're going to do this, do it right.*

Images of her body flashed through his mind as he searched for his case of charcoal pencils. His already-hard penis twitched in anticipation. If he managed to draw her without touching her, he'd become the eighth wonder of the world.

Halfway out the door, he remembered the blanket, yanked the comforter from his bed, and galloped down the stairs with it balled under his arm. He hurried to the conservatory, and upon first glorious sight of her, his feet stopped, along with his heart.

She lay on her back, her rear nestled where the high portion of the chaise met the cushion, calves resting on the furniture back, legs crossed at the ankles. Her head was turned the direction opposite him, as if she were staring out the floor-to-ceiling windows. Her golden hair fanned on the velvet, closest arm dangled toward the floor, and the other stretched above her head. Breasts were more visible than the stars on the clearest south Florida night. And she wasn't wearing panties.

He dropped his bundles on the floor.

She looked toward the ruckus.

His pencil case had opened on impact, and he bent to gather his media. "Sorry. I didn't expect... You surprised me."

"Is this all right?"

"I thought you'd be on your tummy."

She yawned, stretched the entire length of her body, flexed and pointed her toes. Apparently, she'd found her comfort zone. "You already drew my back."

"Just a small part of your back." He was about to close the pencil case but remembered he'd need one to draw with. He selected one and glanced up at her.

She'd already looked back toward the window.

"Sure you don't want a blanket?"

"I'm fine."

Yes, you are. He sat against the doorframe, propped the large sketchbook on his knees, and began to draw. He sketched the outline of her body on the chaise, simple shapes upon shapes, until amalgamated, they became her form.

Usually, he'd start detailing a subject's head and work his way to her feet, or vice versa. But tonight he began in the middle. He rubbed thumbs over two-dimensional nipples and swept charcoal into swollen breasts.

Despite his quick breathing and throbbing groin, he continued his task with patience. Her taut nipples invited his tongue to rove around them. Her belly rose and fell with subtle breaths; he imagined the motion in fast-forward, mid-orgasm, accompanied with a sweet moan of pleasure. *God, this is killing me.*

It wasn't until he sketched the muscle definition of her legs that he realized the suggestion of her position: she looked as if she'd just made love. Tousled and satisfied, yet distant in the way she refused to face him. Her upper body sprawled on the portion of the chaise meant for her feet, as if she'd been positioned and repositioned several times over.

Had she intended to suggest such an interpretation? Or did it exist only in his mind? Perhaps any artist, in any forum, would find her freshly sexed, lying about like that.

With the thought of it, a dull ache plummeted from throat to stomach. He didn't want to share her with other artists—or other men, for that matter. Not when she looked like this.

He scratched a hint of hair between her legs, and jealousy raged within him. How could other artists draw her without wanting her? *That settles it. She poses only for me.*

But he couldn't reserve her, as if she were his property, for the random occasion he might want to crack out a pencil. He wasn't even passionate about drawing; it was just something he did from time to time. It wasn't special. Well, until now, anyway.

Her breasts rose and she sighed in exhalation.

"Oh, Nicki," he whispered.

*   *   *

When he said her name, an insane urge to turn toward him came upon her. She could see his reflection in the glass before her, but she longed to look directly at him to better gauge his expression. He wiped his forehead with the back of his drawing hand and stared at her body. What was he thinking?

His forearms rested against his sketchpad. Why wasn't he drawing her anymore? And why wasn't he speaking? When he finally looked away, he set aside the pad, smeared charcoal from his fingers onto his T-shirt, and left the room.

She held her position. Artists left studios all the time for glasses of water, bathroom breaks. He'd return soon.

Minutes ticked by.

The clapping of a cabinet door against its frame sounded in a distant part of the house, a glass clinked against a surface. No water ran.

She heard footsteps in the hallway, but they did not reach her before they faded.

She closed her eyes, reluctant to move, feeling too beautiful to disrupt her position. And she felt that way in part because of the way he had studied her. She owed it to him to remain motionless.

A few hundred feet away, a boat gurgled past on the intracoastal waterway, and if she concentrated, she could hear the lapping of its wake against boats tethered at the docks.

Where was he? Perhaps he wouldn't return at all, but if he did, she'd be there, just as she had been for over an hour.

Her hands began to tingle. She twitched her fingers to stimulate blood flow and flexed and released each of her muscles without altering her position. The footsteps sounded again. Cool air washed over her skin. He had probably opened a window somewhere.

When she opened her eyes, she saw the reflection of his figure. He stood in the doorway, an open bottle of red wine in one hand, two glasses crisscrossed in the other. He locked his gaze with hers in the window's reflection. "I'm done," he said.

She stretched and arched her back against the chaise. "Can I see it?"

He shook his head and placed the wine and glasses on the floor. "It isn't ready yet."

She swung her legs off the back. "You just said—"

"I'm done for tonight. I can't do any more." He retrieved the comforter from the floor, covered her nude body, and turned back toward the wine.

"We'll finish tomorrow." She readjusted the blanket and cuddled against the cushions.

He shrugged and poured the wine. "Maybe. Want a drink?"

"Sure." She watched him, sensing dread. Had he not found her as intriguing a subject as he thought she'd be? Had her body turned him off? *Damn hips. Too wide, too dominant.*

He sighed heavily and tucked one glass between his ring and pinky fingers and the other between his thumb and index on the same large hand.

"What's wrong?" she asked.

He sat and handed her one of the half-filled glasses. When she reached for the wine, the blanket slipped, revealing the tops of her breasts. But he'd already seen her—all of her—and due to his viewing, beauty coursed through her body like the blood in her veins. After their studio session, making love with him seemed a chance worth taking.

"I was wrong." He brought the glass to his lips, took a long sip, and swallowed slowly. "I can't draw you—hell, I can't look at you—and respect the distance between us." Silence hung in the air. "I'm sorry." He sipped again.

"You covered me." She pulled at the blanket and whisked her bare thigh against his, clad in flannel. "That means you respected the distance."

"I didn't want to."

"But you did."

He looked at her and lowered his forehead to hers. With his forefinger, he raised her chin and positioned her mouth to a perfect location half an inch from his. "You're amazing."

"No, I'm not." *Kiss me, already.*

He traced her bottom lip with his thumb. "I don't deserve this."

The callus on his thumb—so thrilling—traveled across her mouth, caressed her upper lip.

"And you don't need this."

"Yes," she whispered. "I do."

A split second later, his mouth covered hers. With slow precision, their tongues danced together. Tangling, brushing, caressing the taste of red wine into instant heat. He leaned over her and shoved the blanket to the floor. The length of him, warm and virile, pressed against her bare body.

Her mind clouded, but the wine splashing against her shoulder snapped her back to reality. *I'm naked. In south Florida. And Ty's above me.* His glass shattered on the floor and he twisted her hair in his hands. *God, those hands...*

"Limestone's porous," she whispered against his mouth.

"Mmm-hmm." He trailed a hand to one of her breasts.

His hand warmed her chilled skin, plucked at her already alert nipple. His lips lingered at hers, and she felt as if she were floating.

"It'll stain," she breathed, balancing her wineglass.

He gently squeezed her breast, maneuvered a knee between her legs, and pressed his hard penis against her thigh, while his talented mouth captivated her. "I'll put a chair over it," he muttered against her lips.

"You can't put a chair in the middle of the—"

With vigor enough to silence her, he pressed against her and pulled the glass from her hand. It landed on the blanket with a thud, and in her mind, she saw the burgundy liquid bleeding onto the fabric.

"It'll—"

"Nicki?" He kissed her again, wriggled the rest of his body between her thighs, and ground gently against her bare flesh. His gaze pierced into her eyes. "Shut up."

When she wrapped her legs around his waist, she felt each manly inch against her. His drawing hand, moving from her breast to her rear, could have won a Key Award on its own.

By the time she inched the shirt off his well-defined, tan torso and his skin melted onto hers, the smolder between them had grown to a fierce flame. A gruff sigh escaped him, and she couldn't agree more that they felt right together.

He nuzzled her neck, and she bit into his sun-soaked shoulder. *A touch of salt, a dash of aloe.*

A split second later, his thick fingers wriggled against her tender folds, reaching her from behind with a gentle but accurate touch. He kissed her and pressed his hard body against her at the exact moment he plunged a finger inside. She gasped with the coincidence.

His fingers caressed her insides.

Amid the soft breeze filtering through the conservatory and the whispering sensation of his breath at her neck, she felt hot flannel between her fingers. It wasn't until she held him fast and ready in her hand that she realized she had shoved his pants down his hips.

He continued to search her with his fingers, quickening the spinning sensation that clouded her mind. He kissed her again and again, and those full lips alone had talent enough to keep her on her back until sunrise.

Before he slowly dragged a finger out, he pressed another in, over and over. She couldn't keep track of which finger was where, and he worked her with such expertise she no longer cared. When his thumb entered the picture, drawing small circles on a particularly sensitive part inside her, his lips worked at her nipple.

A surge of power rumbled within her. His fingers pressed and pulled and swirled and raked. His thumb brushed and stroked, and pleasure built, built, built.. Tears filled her eyes and fireworks colored her mind until she was a world away. She shivered, fought to catch her breath, but his fingers darted in and out of her, and he was warm against her, and his tongue tickled across her breasts, and...*Oh, my God.*

When her orgasm broke, his lips again traveled to her mouth, and his free hand to her hair. He led her back to reality, to the chaise longue in south Florida, with a calm, controlled kiss and his thumb still circling inside her.

She felt an open-lipped caress on each of her eyes, and then on the tip of her nose. With his thumb nestled inside her and an arm braced against her back, he scooped her up. The member between his legs twitched against her, and she placed a kiss at the corner of his lips, longing to feel him quiver deep inside her.

He carried her through roughly framed walls, up the stairs to his room. His thumb whirled against her one last time as he dragged it out of her, depositing her onto the bed.

"Good night, Nicki Jeanne," He pulled the sheet over their bodies and wrapped his arms around her.

She turned toward him in his embrace, unwilling to sleep before satisfying him, too. His erection, still exposed, now pressed against her stomach.

His eyes were closed and his breathing deep and even, as if he was well on his way to dreamland. But she kissed him anyway, stroked the length of him, and watched for his reaction.

"Hmmm." He placed a hand on hers and returned her kiss. "Another time, kid," he whispered against her lips. "Another time."

CHAPTER 6

In the dim light of daybreak, wearing only the flannel drawstring pants he'd shoved his legs into the night before, Ty leaned against his bedroom wall with a small sketchbook propped against his knees and a charcoal pencil in his grasp.

He stared at Nicki's nude body among disheveled bedclothes. Still unsure of how it had happened, he thought about their heated encounter in the conservatory, and a fiery sensation warmed him from the inside out. He'd drawn her and, overcome with sexual need, he'd left the room and persuaded himself to leave her as untouched as he'd found her. Maybe he should have offered her something less romantic than wine. A beer or a shot of Jaegermeister.

But over the past twenty-one months, she'd grown more beautiful than he imagined possible. It was no wonder he hadn't been able to resist the curve of her hips, her buoyant breasts. She had legs a mile long, the buttocks of a dancer, and the tightest little felix he'd ever pushed his thumb into, but it was the foreign sense of maturity in her eyes he found delectable.

He longed to preserve that wisdom in charcoal. If she were awake, he might be drawing her eyes now, but he had consented to drawing her feet. Something about them had caught his eye when he'd slipped from bed.

Maybe it was the way her feet were positioned: one falling over the other in a comfortable cross formation, a stream of dawn illuminating one, shadowing the other.

Her toe ring, a silver band with a tiny pink stone set in the center, held his attention. Most women wore rings on the second toe, but Nicki wore hers on the fourth. The fact she wore it at all intrigued him because he had never known her to wear jewelry of any kind. It had been reason enough to reach for the closest pencil.

With a thumb, he traced the charcoal arch of her left foot on paper. He'd rather be touching the real thing, but he'd already touched her enough.

And even though she'd responded with verve, he was hardly the man for the job. He was her lifelong friend, not that he'd earned it with honesty of late. The more they shared physically, the more the circumstances regarding Mandy's baby would hurt her.

The sun was nearly up. It was time for him to change clothes and go to work.

He flipped to a blank page in his pad, scribbled a note, and placed it on his pillow. He dragged a finger along her cheek before leaning onto the bed to brush a kiss onto her lips.

She sighed, rolled over, and elbowed his bicep.

*   *   *

The feeling of Ty's hands on her body danced fresh in her mind when she awoke in his bed, sheets twisted about her, not a stitch of clothing on, and she peered at the clock. Just after eight in the morning.

Something crinkled beneath her shoulder. She pulled it out from under her. *Sugar and spice and all things nice.*

Her every muscle ached, a reminder of her physical output the day before—not only on Ty's job site, but on his chaise longue. All things nice indeed. The events of the past twenty-four hours filtered through her mind. The slightest hint of regret nagged at her heart, a paradox against the fulfillment she felt. How could she expect him to believe posing had never before led to a physical encounter, when she had opened up to him like a floodgate?

Her breasts tingled with yearning to feel Ty's hands on her, and the rest of her throbbed with the desire to make love with him. She wouldn't have crossed the line with just anyone. It was Ty on the other side of that sketchpad. But would he see things the same way?

A summery breeze off the intracoastal feathered against her naked body and evoked a feeling of contentment. *Every man on this beach has his eyes on you.* His words of the night before echoed through her mind. *I haven't felt this envied in a long time.*

"Wake up, sweet cheeks." A southern woman's voice, more twang than belle, echoed through the corridors of the lower level.

Nicki froze. Who could that be? A girlfriend? *God, I hope not.* She scrambled to find clothes.

"Hello?" The twang clamored in her ears. "Ty?"

Her heart banged against her ribs, and she reached for the closest article of clothing, which happened to be his discarded pajama pants. They were far too large, but if she pulled the drawstring tight and rolled the waistband down her hips…

"I brought breakfast, sugar-pie."

Nicki scanned the area. *Shirt, shirt, shirt.* Of course, none of *her* things were strewn about—she remembered with a wince that she had yet to unpack—but she spied the shirt he'd worn to dinner last night. She yanked it out from half-under the bed and threw it on. Her wearing Ty's clothes would look suspicious if the woman downstairs was, in fact, a Fort Lauderdale love interest, but it was better than being caught in the raw in his bedroom.

"I hear you scuttling about up there."

Nicki frantically fastened only one button and tied the remaining shirttails into a sloppy square knot above her navel.

"Do I need to come up there and rouse you?"

She raced into the bathroom, ran Ty's wire hairbrush through her hair and a fingerful of cinnamon-flavored toothpaste over her teeth. There was one advantage to never putting anything away—everything was accessible.

"Do you like orange muffins?" the woman asked from below. "I always forget."

Nicki rushed down the stairs, unsure how she was going to explain her presence.

"What on earth did you do to this room last night?"

Following the sound of the voice, Nicki wove through stud-walls, around stacks of tumbled marble tile, until she spotted an older woman wearing a turquoise bikini and an orange fishnet cover-up standing in the doorway of the conservatory.

"Hi."

The guest spun around and smiled, revealing a smudge of hot-pink lipstick on her teeth. She spread her arms and stepped toward her. The revealing shirt did nothing to conceal the surprisingly fit, though aged, body beneath it. "You must be Nicki."

Nicki began to nod, and the woman hugged her.

"I'm Verna." She placed balled fists onto her hips and looked again into the conservatory. "Hum. I wonder."

"He dropped a glass last night," Nicki said.

The guest waved at the mess and wiggled through a doorway. "So where is our charming guy?"

"He had to work." She followed at the other woman's heels to a room that resembled the remains of a kitchen.

There was no flooring installed, although boxes on boxes of what appeared to be an amber-colored tile—terra cotta, maybe—were stacked near an atrium door at the far side of the room. Horrid, green paisley wallpaper covered two walls, interrupted only by masses of an equally disturbing baby blue paint, where cabinets once hung. *This is the first room I'm going to tackle.* Dull pain raced through her biceps. *Assuming I can muster the strength.*

"Work? On a Sunday? If I'd known that, I wouldn't have woke you. But here. Have a muffin, Tinkerbell." Verna leaned onto a makeshift countertop, a sheet of plywood that bridged a free-standing cabinet and a box labeled wet-dry vac, and gave the green glass platter before her a tiny shove. "They're orange, of course, but what isn't in this state? We're flipping proud of our oranges, I'll tell you that much."

"Thanks." Nicki selected one with a generous top mound and began to peel off the baking cup.

"Sex does tend to make a gal hungry." Verna puckered her lips and shifted her sunglasses atop her head.

Nicki glanced at her, and then back to her muffin, unsure how she should react, and even whether or not she should react at all.

"Sweetheart, sex ain't nothing to be ashamed of." With the shake of Verna's head a few strands of straight, obviously dyed jet-black hair fell from a clip that resembled two chopsticks and a fortune cookie. "Especially with a hunk of a man like Ty. Now waking up next to what sacked me last night..." She shrugged. "Well, that's a different story. Don't get me wrong. Once upon a time, I'm sure my beau was Paul Newman-in-his-prime, but I tell you this: he ain't much but an occasional hard-on these days."

She picked up a muffin and perused it before peeling off the paper. "Enjoy it while it lasts, honey." Verna tapped extra long, acrylic fingernails against the plywood. "And I bet that boy can last and last."

"Um..." *How am I supposed to respond to that?* Nicki gave her head a slight shake, just enough to shift her curls. "I understand you used to own this house."

"Yup. Used to be a rental with two units."

"Really?" She glanced around the room. Kitchens were usually back-to-back in rentals. That would explain the header buried in the cut-open ceiling. There used to be a wall dividing the vast space. "Did you gut it? Or Ty?"

"I don't know a damn thing about restoration." Verna fished a wad of purple gum out of her mouth with a fingernail and pressed it onto the platter. "All this is Ty's vision. Kinda makes you wonder what it is he's seeing, don't it?"

Whatever his vision, Nicki knew it would be fabulous, but before she could offer her own opinion, Verna was talking again.

"My George liked to rent to pretty little things. 'Who should I grace with my presence today? The slut in number one? Or the hussy in number two?' It's a wonder we spent any time together at all, now I think about it."

"I'm sorry?"

"You heard right. That son of a bitch was uglier than sin itself, but that sure-as-shooting didn't stop him. Two houses down the street we lived on, and he thought I wouldn't hear tell." She clenched a hand into a fist and looked to hell. "Do you hear me, George Davis? I don't know how you found your way between so many pretty sets of legs, looking the way you did." Sighing heavily, she again looked to Nicki. "Men. I'm starting to think you can shoot 'em after all."

Nicki opened her mouth, but quickly clamped it shut. No appropriate response existed in the realm of her imagination.

"Don't pay it no mind." Verna bit into her muffin. "Sounds like you been through quite an ordeal yourself."

Nicki pulled the sleeve over the bruise on her wrist. "I'm all right."

"You've got Ty in knots."

"What else is new?"

"You must be one special chickadee for him to be biting his nails. Considering all he's got on his own plate. That boy's so worried about his own situation he's kept to himself more in the past few months since..." Verna pressed her lips together. "No, no. It ain't my business."

"Since what?"

Verna pursed her lips. "I shouldn't have said a word. It's a problem, I know. I talk too much, scatter too much gossip." She stuck her fingernail into the wad of chewed gum on the platter and bit it back into her mouth. "No, sirree. I'll let Ty fill you in. Thought he was going to last night, but…like I said. Men. How long are you staying, dumpling?"

"I'm not sure."

"How about you and me hitting the beach? I'll show you around the broadwalk, take you to some shops along the boulevard."

"I only wish. I need to settle in and clean today. Rain check?"

Verna shook her head and swallowed a mouthful of muffin. "You don't wanna spend your first day in south Florida inside."

"I don't have a choice. I can't live like this." She scanned her surroundings. "How can anyone?"

"That's the magic of the locale, honey bunny. Who cares what you have inside, when outside, everything's coming up roses?" The older woman drummed acrylics against the counter. "Anyway, if you change your mind, come find me. I've got a great pool down the street a piece at number thirty-one, and ain't no one on this isle against skinny dipping. It's better for a tan, you know. Swimming naked means no unsightly lines, except those you earn with age."

"I'll remember that."

Verna straightened and headed for the door. "And put some shoes on before you cut those sexy toes off. Lord knows what you might step on in this dungeon."

"Verna?" Nicki raked through her hair and followed her guest to the door. "I don't suppose you can loan me a gallon of bleach?"

"You might need something stronger to cut through the grime of this joint—like whiskey. To imbibe, not scrub with. But sure, I think I can find something. I'll bring it by with lunch in a few hours. It'll take you at least that long to sweep up the layers of dust." With a wink, she was gone.

*   *   *

Ten miles from the Isle of Venice and one story up, Ty raised another wall and concealed a smile.

When he'd arrived that morning, Joe Montalvo had been there, scratching his head over the tub deck roughed in for the whirlpool. "Couldn't sleep this morning," Montalvo had said. "The deck's not right."

"No room for the faucet," they'd said together.

Ty hadn't planned on spending more than an hour at the site, but they'd been making progress, working together. And the fact Montalvo had shown up, without coercion, on a Sunday…well, it could only mean good things in finishing the house in time to qualify for the Key Award—maybe even Custom Homebuilder of the Year.

The journeyman sat on a personal-sized cooler and peeled a banana in the blazing sun. "Heard Mandy hired a lawyer."

Ty pulled a cordless nail gun from his belt. "Who told you?"

"The whole crew heard her talking the other day. It's no secret."

"Great." Ty began to toe-nail the frame into place, in hope the cacophony would deter any further discussion.

"So what're you going to do?" Montalvo asked. He wiped a hand across his brow, and bit into the banana.

"The same thing you're doing right now. Nothing."

"Is it true? That baby yours?"

"If you're going to sit around and gab, you might as well go home to your family. I'm done talking about it." He turned back to his task. Thwack, thwack, thwack. He'd have to talk about it eventually. If not in the court of law, in the forum of his own home, with Nicki.

He should tell her the truth, if he expected her to stay. But is that what he wanted? After the events in the conservatory, he felt compelled to ask.

He tried to tell himself everything sexual had stemmed from his drawing her, and that hadn't been his idea. His thumb wound up inside of her as a consequence to a decision she made. She'd drenched his hand; he'd restrained himself from exploding into her, which was among the most difficult things he'd ever done. But he'd done it, and as long as he continued to stick to that plan, the playing field would slope to his advantage.

There were several problems with that train of thought, however.

First of all, things had become sexual the moment she set foot on south Florida soil. Even without that inexplicable moment at the job site when he'd almost kissed her, without the invitation to draw her, sex steamed between them, instantly and inevitably.

Second, he didn't want to put her at a disadvantage. She wasn't just any girl. She was the one he'd always taken care of. He shouldn't think of their relationship in terms of playing fields, keeping score, and who had the ball in whose court. He respected her too much for that, and he wanted what was best for her.

And third, the prospect of loving Nicki made him realize he was tired of playing altogether.

*　　*　　*

Nicki swept, scrubbed, and polished. Stacked, moved, and filed. The bruise on her wrist, a reminder of duct tape and imprisonment, ached with every flex of her wrist. As much as its presence degraded her, it also empowered her. She was no man's property; she made her own decisions, and she'd chosen Fort Lauderdale.

She entered the conservatory with a bucket and scrub brush and stepped over the dress she'd removed last night. A rumpled puddle on the floor, it warmed her heart with the memory of a nervous Ty Carmichael, sliding the zipper down her back, his lips lingering at her mouth...and red wine seeping into the limestone. *Hope that stain comes out.*

She dropped to her hands and knees and scoured the limestone with bleach. *Hmm. Move that doorway two or three feet, and we can accommodate built-in corner hutches in the dining room. And pocket doors with true-light mullions in the conservatory will draw sunlight further into the home.*

Her glance trailed to the worn chaise longue, and she lifted her face to the balmy breeze that swept in off the intracoastal.

*   *   *

Ty opened the door to a clean, organized job site and backed onto the porch again. He lifted the Three-peat hat from his head and looked at the mailbox. Number twenty-five, Isle of Venice Drive. Sure enough, this was his home. He hesitated for a moment before pulling the cap back over his hair and peeking through the doorway.

Yes, his home was clean.

And, yum. It smelled like tomato sauce.

"Nicki?" His voice echoed throughout the first level, and he took a cautious step inside.

What the hell? His makeshift workbench was now located in the front room. Random tools, including three lost tape measures and a hammer he hadn't seen in a month, lined the top. Okay, so she'd found a few things. Did she really expect him to walk all the way to the front of the house when he was working on the rooms in the back? He'd put that workbench in the kitchen for a reason, and he'd probably put the newfound hammer in some unknown place with a motive in mind. He just couldn't remember what that motive was right now.

Countless boxes of tile sat, neatly stacked, in the corner. So, she'd swept and washed the sub-floor. So, it was clean enough to lay naked on. He wasn't supposed to *lay* on it, he was supposed to lay *tile* on it.

Now he had to lug all those heavy boxes back into the kitchen when the time came to install, and... He looked down at his feet—and at the dirt now scattered in a three-inch radius around them.

He shoved off his work boots and carried them back to the foyer, following the trail he'd left on his way in. He might have tried to sweep it up, but it was a useless task. More would shake off his clothing anyway.

Women. Why couldn't they see that function was a role as important as beauty when it came to constructing homes? And how was he supposed to keep his quarters clean running a miter saw, or worse yet, sanding drywall? Cleanliness might have seemed nice in her head, but it was as impractical in the field as a twenty-one-inch-wide doorway: a person could squeeze through, but he'd have nothing inside to sit on because a chair wouldn't make it past the threshold.

"Nicki?" He walked through the dining room, which now housed bundles of two-by-fours and panels of sheetrock and plywood. How the hell had she moved all that on her own? *So help me, if she enlisted the help of that jackass from Hendricks, I'll—*

The aroma of something Italian grew robust, and he stopped in his tracks. He could forgive her for rearranging his space in exchange for good food.

He caught sight of her. Hell, he'd forgive her if he could stare at her for a while. She was standing over a small section of countertop that once had been home to countless tools, engrossed in a swatch of graph paper and wearing one of his flannel shirts—the blue-and-gray plaid one with the rip just under the lowest button. The sleeves were rolled to her forearms, the shirttails hit her legs mid-thigh, and, when she leaned onto the countertop, something red and enticing peeked at him from between the buttons at her cleavage.

A cloud of blonde curls and the aroma of a rose sachet hung about her, drawing him near, daring him to touch her, smell her, taste her.

When he was less than twelve inches away, she looked up with wide eyes and, after a second, returned her attention to the paper on the counter. "Hi, bright eyes. How was your day?"

"Hot." He forced his glance away from her breasts, which did more than justice to his grungy, old shirt.

But the sight of her drew his gaze again. Her clean skin shimmered in the incandescent light, as if she'd sprinkled a pinch of gold dust into whatever lotion she'd applied that day, and her toenails were painted red to match what little clothing he suspected he'd find beneath the flannel.

He breathed in the soft scent of roses and took a step back to avoid dropping her to the kitchen floor. "Do I smell flowers?"

"Maybe." She bounced the pencil twice against her full bottom lip and then pointed it toward the bundle of seven roses he'd given her yesterday evening, now bound and hanging upside down in his kitchen window.

But the already-faint perfume waned as he stepped away from her. It was her, all right. Her dangerous, all-consuming combination of fruit and flowers was going to be the death of him. His heart pounded, and the muscle between his legs began to harden. "Toes look nice," he said, just above a whisper.

"Thanks." She didn't take her eyes from the paper. "Ever going to retire that hat?"

"No." He looked at the stove and noticed the oven light illuminating a rectangular casserole dish. "Are you cooking?"

"Yes."

"How'd you manage that?"

"I connected the range. Verna and I found the gas valve."

"Smells good."

"Thanks. Verna bought too much at the Dania Beach Tomato Festival. Thus, Italian."

He nodded, not that she was looking to see it. "Do I have time for a shower?"

"Mmm-hmm. Let me know if that tub's shiny enough for you, and prepare to hand over those car keys."

He lingered in the doorway for a few moments, detecting the smile in her words, although she was too engrossed in her drawing to express it. "You didn't have to clean, you know."

"I beg to differ."

Sweat ran like a river down his back and chest, and his T-shirt stuck to his skin. But still he delayed, as if she might fade away during his absence. He wanted to brush against her body, cover her with his hard-earned sweat, and see where such contact might lead them, but he didn't dare kiss her hello.

She seemed focused on her sketching, but perhaps her distance was due to regret. He'd been so preoccupied with his own feelings about the chaise longue that he'd neglected to wonder how she felt about it.

She'd been into it last night all right, but the heat of that moment could have persuaded a born-again virgin to give it up. And how sweet her surrender had been—her body writhing beneath his, her scrumptious lips tearing at his mouth, her breasts tickling against his chest, her thighs tightening as she reached climax.

He took the steps two at a time and raced to the shower. *Cold water, cold water, cold water.* He should think of something besides her body. But what could distract him from the memory of the orgasm he'd stroked out of her last night?

Think about the mess with Mandy. That'll deflate your ego. And other things, too. Mandy, Mandy, Mandy. Oh, good. It's working.

Worse case scenario, it would be a headache-and-a-half to comply with testing. So why wasn't he taking Verna's advice? A simple blood test could end it all.

Or it could start a lifetime of responsibility. Maybe it wasn't a matter of counting weeks. Maybe the doctor *was* wrong about the due date.

But he'd used protection. Every time. And if the doctor was off, he was four weeks off, and that wasn't very likely. Or was it? Maybe Nicki would know more about that stuff.

But could he ask her?

How would she react to the news? In a practical manner…perhaps. She wasn't as naïve as he had, until recently, preferred to believe.

He remembered her sprawled body on the chaise, her vigorous response to his touch, the tiny catch in her breath just before she came.

And her mouth was talented. He'd kiss her all night, if he wasn't so hell-bent on feeling those luscious lips around his…

Damn. Did every thought lead to sex with her? He turned the water colder.

Wait a minute. His Betty Boop shower curtain was gone, replaced with the slick white one he'd kept, in its original package, under the sink. All right, so Betty was dingier than hell, but she was his. He'd always had a soft spot for the sexy cartoon. She possessed the perfect combination of class and sass, not unlike her namesake, his car. And now Nicki had eliminated one of his Bettys.

That's it. The tub looks out-of-a-showroom shiny, but she's never driving my car.

By the time his shower was over, he had fallen to half-mast. He opened the bottom dresser drawer for a pair of boxer shorts, only to be greeted by the smell of roses. She'd left a note: *Top drawer in the highboy.*

Apparently, she'd reorganized more than his tools. No one—not even Nicki—had the right to shuffle through his underwear drawer, even though he'd been in her drawers. He pressed a hand to a neat pile of silky garments, intending to shove the drawer closed, but the familiar scent of roses floated up and stopped him cold.

His irritation faded and he again crushed his fingers into the silk. It wasn't the drying bouquet he'd smelled in the kitchen. It was her lingerie. God help him, he couldn't ignore the pull of their bodies forever.

He meandered across the room to the highboy. It made more sense to keep his clothing there anyway. Closer to the bathroom, it was a stop on the way to the closet. He stepped into a pair of boxers, shoved his way into a T-shirt, and then felt beneath the pile.

There it was—the ring box. Next to the condoms. Well, at least she was thorough. She'd moved everything.

At random, he pulled a pair of neatly folded shorts from the second drawer and put them on, in mid-stride, on his way to the hallway.

He entered the kitchen just in time to avoid bumping into his organization specialist as she pulled a casserole from the oven, but his little finger grazed against the edge of the pan.

"Damn it!" He snapped his hand away and muttered obscenities under his breath.

"Make some noise next time, will you?" She slid the concoction onto the stovetop and shook free from an old oven mitt. "Did I burn you?"

"No, it tickles." He refused to look at her, lifting his finger to his mouth.

She intercepted, took a hard look at the tiny, red welt, and wrapped her tongue around his finger

For the first time, he noticed the flecks of gold in her brown irises and their amber rims. Her tongue massaged his finger, and pleasure darted through his entire body. He tensed in her grip. "I'm all right, Nicki."

Her tongue curled against his finger with unyielding suction, and her lips puckered at the base of his knuckle. There was no doubting it now: he had to be buried in that mouth to his hilt. And soon. He felt the talent of her tongue throughout his body, and the heat of her sexuality spread like wildfire in his veins. So much for half-mast now.

She dragged her lips off his finger, still staring into his eyes. "I'm sorry."

"I'm all right," he managed to say.

She turned back to the range and switched off the oven. "It's baked ziti. You owe Verna half a pound of ricotta, but interestingly enough, you had almost everything else. What you were planning to do with a box of..."

He couldn't concentrate on her words. Only on the way the flannel threatened to slide off her perfect shoulder, the way it flowed like a cotton wave against her ass and thighs when she moved about the ramshackle room.

Worse—or better, depending on the point of view—he could still feel the suction of her tongue against his finger, which led to thoughts of oral pleasure of another kind. He closed his eyes, breathed deeply, but he couldn't escape the image of her body.

"Nicki." He opened his eyes. "What was that?"

She turned toward him and extended a glass of wine, poured from the bottle they'd made a dent in the night before. "What's what?"

"The finger trick." He fixated on her eyes, and when he drew in a long breath, raspberry-vanilla air filled his lungs. He took a step toward her.

"I don't know."

He accepted the wine and set it aside, too preoccupied with her mouth to thank her.

"The cold water doesn't work in here." She turned toward the pan of ziti, and the shirt slipped off her shoulder, revealing a lacy, red bra strap. "And the next closest tap is—"

In one quick motion, he pulled her into his arms and kissed her. He pressed against her, cupped her backside—*God, she's bare beneath*—and lifted her to the counter top, where she had been drawing. "Three suitcases," he breathed into her ear, "and not a pair of panties to spare?"

"I'm wearing—"

He kissed her again, trailed a hand to her toes, and fingered the ring around the fourth. His other hand meandered between her thighs, and the same pinky finger she had sucked on brushed against a tiny string of a thong. So she was wearing panties after all. Just not much to them.

*   *   *

A low hum registered in her ear when he nibbled on her lobe, and the familiar prelude to sex swept through her like an aggressive wave. The memory of Ty's magical thumb sent a surge of pleasure pulsing through her so fast she almost surrendered to his little finger. But in a brief bout of sanity, she pressed her hands against his chest. "Ty."

He kissed her one last time and backed away an inch, his finger dawdling. His eyes seemed bluer than normal, ignited with passion.

"I have to serve dinner," she murmured.

"I'll serve you instead." He bit his lower lip and reclaimed her mouth.

"I don't sleep with the students who draw me," she whispered against his lips and, cupped his face in her hands.

"I think we covered that last night."

"I did a poor job of proving it." She attempted to slide off the countertop, but he leaned into her with another kiss.

"Mmm." He squeezed her at the bend between her thigh and hip. "Who says you did a poor job of anything?"

"A serving pantry. That's it."

"What?"

She slid to the floor and spun toward the countertop, his body still encircling hers, his hands planted on either side of her on the counter. His erection grazed against her lower back.

"Look!" She glanced at him over her shoulder and shifted the graph paper she'd been sitting on. "This section of the kitchen's been bothering me all day. It's too awkward a spot to be useful. As you were good enough to demonstrate, an oven shouldn't open in this doorway for safety reasons, and it's too far away from the sink for convenience.

"But if we build out a wall here"—she reached for a pencil and sketched over previously drawn lines—"and here, we'll have an independent pantry between the kitchen and dining room. An original Ty Carmichael pastel on this wall, opposite tall, glass-door cabinets where you can keep things like platters, large bowls, and serving pieces. Not that you have any, but you might someday, provided you find the right—"

He raked her hair across her shoulders and placed a soft, wet kiss on her neck. "Genius." He melted another kiss on her shoulder. "What else do you have in mind?"

Traditional china. No black-stemmed, art deco glassware for us. Her eyes flickered open, and until then, she hadn't known she'd closed them. He was good at what he did. Too good. Distracting. And she'd planned a distraction of her own for after they'd eaten. "Dinner." She slipped out from under him. "I thought we'd eat in the garden and watch the boats go by. There's a table out there."

"I know. I put it there." He shifted his shorts. "So what's with the panties? Or should I say lack thereof?"

70

Heat crawled into her cheeks.

"You couldn't have worn something that wouldn't turn me on? Something cotton and shapeless?"

She tugged on the collar of the flannel shirt. "This is cotton and shapeless."

"No, it isn't. This…" He waved a hand in her direction, toe to head. "This is cruel. I'm trying to do the right thing and there's nothing sexier, believe me, than the suggestion of what you're wearing. Looks like you rolled over, pulled on the first thing you saw, and—"

"—just rolled out of bed. Thanks."

"You know what I mean. It looks like we just… like we…" He stared at her, the same look in those precious blue eyes as she'd seen the night before, just before his thumb sent her skydiving through pleasure.

"And there it is again," he said. "That little something mysterious peeking out at me. It just makes me want to see more. You know that."

No, she hadn't known. She'd planned on dropping the shirt in an hour or two, but with this reaction, she might keep it on.

He turned toward the cupboard and opened a creaking door, only to close it again. "Where'd you put the plates?"

"Closer to the sink, where they should be."

He sighed and headed across the room. "According to whom?"

"Anyone who's ever washed a dish. Why take twenty steps to put it away?"

"You learned too much, working for my father."

"Apparently, not enough."

He opened another cabinet and selected two mismatched dinner plates.

She was suddenly too nervous to eat, but she allowed him to heap baked ziti onto the plates. "Listen, I was just out of the shower and I had to check on dinner, so I grabbed the closest shirt, which happened to be yours." She inched closer to him, dared to touch his elbow. "I put all my things in the back of the closet, out of your way."

He looked at her, but offered no reply aside from a deep breath.

She nearly forgot what she was saying, so intense was his stare. A curious force within her had her gravitating even closer to him. "And you've seen me in things like this before, and—"

"Before was a lifetime ago."

"I didn't mean to… Not yet, any—"

His mouth met hers in an unexpected kiss.

*   *   *

Wow! The things she could do to him.

He dropped the serving spoon into the casserole, pulled her closer still, and deepened the kiss.

So she didn't mean to disrupt his life. He didn't mean to want her. But hell, they didn't stand a chance with attraction exploding between them like Vesuvius.

He squeezed the left cheek of her rear and pressed every inch of her against him. Her breasts crushed against his chest with precision, and the heat of her purred against his thighs, beckoning him to her with a hot whisper.

"I want to be in there," he breathed against her lips, even as he tucked a thumb into her thong.

Her fingers slid through his damp hair, scrunching and pulling, and a sweet moan of pleasure rang in his ears. When her hand plunged into his shorts, a dizzying sensation whirled around him. He backed her into a doorway, lifted her against a naked two-by-four, and wriggled his fingers under her panties.

A breath shuddered against his mouth, and the hand in his pants moved from his testicles to the tip of his penis with a slow, thorough stroke before maneuvering his shorts out of the way. Two firm thighs pressed around his hips when she locked her legs around him.

He imagined her heat surrounding his shaft, her wet channel pulsing against him. He shouldn't make love to her, but oh, if he could… She broke their kiss to yank his shirt over his head, but quickly bit into his mouth again as if he were an apple hanging ripe.

He anticipated she'd grind against him, drip around him, pull an orgasm out of him like soda through a straw. If he wasn't careful, it might happen too soon. Her thighs tightened around his waist.

"Let me in there." He pulled at her thong. Her taut nipples grazed against his chest, through her clothing. "Let me in."

"How much more in can you be?" Her hands pressed against his cheeks, and he focused on her dreamy eyes, lit with a sexual fire. He caught his breath.

She rolled her hips in a slow gyration, holding his gaze all the while. He hadn't imagined her grinding, her dripping around him. He hadn't imagined it at all. Somehow, during his cloudy musings, he'd taken her. He was in there all right. Making love to her despite their history—and her tiny panties.

"Left pocket," she breathed.

He reached into the pocket of her shirt and extracted a red foil package. "You're dangerous." He pushed himself deeper into her, ran a hand under the flannel, up her side, and cupped a breast. The lace of her brassiere felt soft against the calluses on his fingers. What was he thinking? What was he doing? "We shouldn't."

She nodded, biting her bottom lip.

"Not like this." He pulled out, lowered her feet to the floor, and pressed the condom into her hand. "I've never wanted anything more, but—"

"That makes two of us." She tore the package open with her teeth and unrolled the latex over his cock with swift hands.

Double wow. He swung her around and sank to the freshly washed plywood sub-floor. She slid onto him, straddling him, moving in small circles. Woman on top.

He trailed a hand along her bruised spine, hoping the wall hadn't done any further damage. He unhooked her brassiere and, with a gentle pressure, he hugged her closer.

"Better?" He tunneled through the flannel and massaged the curls at the nape of her neck.

She nodded. "Perfect."

He laced a thumb into her thong and ripped. She melted full against him, free from the panties, and their tongues entwined with a simultaneous gasp.

He held her to him, rocked into her and out again. Slow and steady. And each time he pushed in, her vagina gripped and stroked the length of him, pulling him deeper and deeper, all the while dripping like honey off a hive.

She ripped open buttons on the flannel shirt, freeing her arms, pulling at her bra and baring her breasts. The sight of them, bouncing free, sent a shiver of joy straight to his cock. He closed his eyes to ground himself. *Don't come, don't come, don't come yet.*

Instinctively, he brought his mouth to one full, beautiful mound, rolling his tongue around her nipple. She tasted every bit as sweet as she smelled and as glorious as she felt.

Not twenty-four hours ago, he'd recreated those breasts in charcoal, and now, they rested against him, in his mouth, in his hands. And the valley between her thighs, which remained a mystery in his sketchbook, he now knew more than intimately. He knew where to find the most tender spots inside her, and he memorized the right rhythm, the beat that would carry her all the way there.

With every stroke, her fingers gripped and scratched his shoulders. Her sweat mingled with his, their tongues tangled. *Not yet.*

She tensed in his arms, kneaded against his hips, and her breath shuddered in a staccato exhalation. As her climax gushed hot and sweet around him, she kissed him with abandoned hunger.

He wove his hands into her hair. *Now.*

CHAPTER 7

From her position astride him on the kitchen floor, she looked into his eyes. "Did you just…"

His penis pulsated, hot and thick inside her.

"Sorry about the wall." He fingered her curls. His voice sounded gruff, satisfied, if not sleepy. "I don't know what I was thinking. You all right?"

"A bit better than all right."

He pushed his hips up against her while pressing down on her backside and groaned. "God, you feel good."

"You, too." She brushed a blond strand from his forehead.

"Come here." He kissed her again.

She felt as warm and safe in his arms in the aftermath of lovemaking as she had during. He'd loved her meticulously. Somehow, he'd managed to hit every nerve at just the right time. "Better than I ever imagined."

"So incredibly right." He thrust into her again and tickled her up her spine. "Wasn't it?" His kiss silenced her before she agreed, and she shivered with the reality of what had just happened, pleasure continually darting through her body. Their noses rubbed together.

"Dinner's getting cold," she said.

"Dinner." He smiled. "I am pretty hungry."

*   *   *

He found her torn panties—Secret Notions Kissed Collection—and rubbed their silky remains between his fingers, studying her. He had a pretty good idea of what had happened in Chicago, and unthinkable as it was, she was the picture of composure, considering what they'd just done.

Her dainty fingers popped buttons through button holes, and she shook her damp curls from the collar of her shirt as if she didn't have a care in the world. There it was again, that collected, controlled look of wisdom in her eyes, proving she was no longer the naïve girl he'd left behind.

Neither of them spoke as they gathered their plates and carried them to the wrought iron bistro table in the garden.

Silence did not seem to bother her, but it sure as hell bothered him. How had she pulled herself together so quickly? Didn't she know what had just happened? They'd made love—toe-curling, Richter-scale-registering love. *They* did. Old friends, new lovers.

"Are you going to join me?" she asked from her chair. She opened a napkin on her lap. "Or are you going to stand there and watch me eat?"

He felt a corner of his mouth twitch and sat at the table among overgrown hibiscus and colitis. A gecko scrambled across a flagstone path and up the trunk of a palm tree, pausing for a second as if examining her, too. The usual tranquility of the garden did not exist at that moment; the serenity of the waterway did nothing to calm his heartbeat.

She was turning his life topsy-turvy, and it had been plenty skewed before she'd arrived. She played tricks with his body, rearranged his house, and now she was messing with his mind.

"How long are you staying?" He didn't know he'd spoken until he heard his own voice ringing in his ears.

"I don't know. I didn't plan that far ahead. I just…I needed to leave, so I left."

He nodded. Had she moved in? She'd certainly brought enough luggage to last half a year.

"I didn't know this would happen when I came here." She dabbed the corners of her mouth with her napkin and reached for his hand. "I have a life back in Chicago, with house plants, a run-down apartment, and a roommate who's going to be thoroughly ticked off when she realizes I'm gone. And I'm supposed to be in front of thirty students at six tomorrow evening in Studio C. I haven't forgotten."

"I didn't say you did."

A breeze whisked between their bodies, billowing her shirt. He couldn't resist looking between the lapels, glimpsing her swollen breasts, nearly bursting out of the bra.

"If I'd thought posing for you would lead to—"

"Nicki, I didn't draw you so I could make love to you, and I didn't make love to you because I drew you."

"Stranger things have happened."

His glance strayed from hers, but he looked back after a moment, tapping his fork against his plate of untouched ziti. "I don't know what happened to you in Chicago, but my kitchen floor wasn't about our session last night."

"What was it about then?"

"Can you, for once, answer a question without asking one?"

"I don't think I heard one." She raised an eyebrow. "Have you ever been engaged?"

"Damn it, Nicki." He dropped his fork and challenged her with a steady stare.

"Just tell me. Have you ever been engaged?"

"Why?"

"I was wondering whose ring I found in your T-shirt drawer."

"*Quid pro quo*, kid."

She sipped her wine and licked her lips. The breeze tossed her hair, and, for a moment, she looked as she had on the chaise longue— tousled, thoroughly sated, mysteriously distant.

"We both have questions," he said. "It's fair play."

"Fine. Ask."

"Whatever happened in Chicago wasn't consensual, was it?"

Her brow furrowed, and he brushed his thumb over her fingers in encouragement. She shook her head. "No, it wasn't something I agreed to, but—"

"Even if he was your fiancé, if you said no—"

"They didn't get that far."

"They?" He tightened his grip on her fingers. "What happened?"

Her eyes widened, she drew a deep breath, and just when he thought she'd answer him, she again shook her head. "*Quid pro quo.* Did I interrupt something by coming here?"

"I guess you could say that, but not in the way you think."

"In what way then?"

"My turn: You said 'they.' Explain that."

"You don't want to know."

"No, I don't, but as it stands, I don't have a choice, do I?"

She wiggled her fingers in his hand, staring out at the water. "I'm fine."

"Well, I'm not. What happened?"

"He always thought it might be fun to bring in a third, just to watch, he said. But he didn't get that far."

"He didn't get far enough to rape you. How far did he get?"

"Far enough to scare me."

"Far enough to bruise you."

"That, too."

"And this is the man you agreed to marry?"

"Who agreed to marry *you*?"

"No one. I never asked her."

"The ring—"

"—was my Great Aunt Evie's. The one thing I fought my sisters for when she died, and I've had it for over a decade."

"Still, there was someone you meant to ask?"

"Did he toss you around? Hit you?"

"Hit me? No. Toss me around, yes. Duct taped me to the door, bit me and drew blood, shoved me against a slab of dakota mahogany granite…" She shook her head.

His heart sank and his mouth instantly dried. "I can't imagine…"

"He liked to push me, that's all. To see how far I'd go, to see what I'd do for him."

He swallowed hard and looked away. "Was that the only time?"

Two soft fingers tugged up his chin, luring his gaze back to her. "I'm all right," she whispered. The flannel slipped off her shoulder.

What gorgeous bone structure. To think anyone would exploit a body like that… He looked to his plate, unsure whether he wanted to ask the next question. He glanced at her to find she had yet to look away. She was a strong woman, and at the moment, he was a gambling man. "Do you still love him?"

"Well, that's disturbing, too." She ran a finger around the rim of the wineglass. "The second I walked out that door, I couldn't remember loving him at all. Diabolical, isn't it?"

"Not after going through all that."

"I think I loved the idea more. Not being alone all the time, having someone. And he seemed sensible, stable. Artsy, too. He works at a gallery."

"But this is exactly why I want you to stop modeling. Some idiot is always going to assume you deserve to be used."

She rolled her eyes and over-dramatized a yawn. "Let's talk about you and what's-her-name."

"Who?"

"The girl you almost thought about maybe asking to marry you."

"Mandy Washington."

"I'm assuming she's the secretary?"

He nodded.

"And you wanted to marry her?"

"Never." He shrugged. "Well, maybe for a minute, but it was a short minute. A long time ago."

"That serious, huh?" Her smile struck like lightning, illuminating her eyes, and she giggled, perching a foot on the seat of her chair.

The urge almost overcame him to drop to the ground and taste her beneath the table. After all, she wasn't wearing panties, and only a flimsy flannel shirttail with a rip in it covered the treasure between her legs.

"Too much sage?" She lifted a forkful of ziti to his mouth.

He took the offered morsel and smiled, picking up his own fork. "Oh, it's terrible."

"Thanks."

"Now about my shower curtain."

"I don't want to hear it. How you've pulled that rank vinyl around you for two years I'll never know."

"I liked Betty."

"Do you like fungus, too? Because she was covered in it. I scrubbed and scrubbed, but it was there to stay."

"The place looks great, but how did you move all those heavy things into the—"

"Some guy from Hendricks Isle offered to give me a hand, so—"

"Tabor?"

"I didn't catch his name, but Verna knows him."

"Dark hair, more brawn than height?" *Slept with my ex-girlfriend and won't take responsibility for the consequence.*

"Sounds about right. Good looking guy, a little full of himself."

"That's him. What did he tell you?"

"Nothing."

"Good. But in the future, don't talk to him. And don't believe a word he says."

"He said he helps you sometimes—"

"Well, he doesn't."

"I needed help lugging enough sheetrock up the stairs to those bedrooms. Verna couldn't do it, so I took him up on his offer to help."

He ground his teeth and gave his head a shake, attempting to chase away a nagging in his stomach. He was jealous, he didn't like it, and the thought of her being alone in a bedroom with that jerk…"He was hitting on you, Nicki."

"So what? He did a lot of work, and he didn't get anywhere." She flashed a grin. "We came out ahead."

"Next time, don't play the game. Call him on it."

"Here, try this." Calm and composed, she spooned parmesan cheese over his entrée. "Be honest. Did I use too much basil?"

"No."

"Really, it's too—"

"Perfect," he said. Her smile hit him right in the heart. "Too perfect." Dinner was perfect, sex with her was perfect, and yes, even his new shower curtain and organized underwear drawer were perfect.

"I'm such a lucky girl, you know that?"

Lucky? If only she knew what she was getting herself into.

CHAPTER 8

An elbow pierced him between the shoulder blades, jolting him from a hazy sleep. He squinted through the sandy crust in his eyes at the neon green numbers on his clock. Five-forty-three in the morning.

He rolled toward Nicki, about to envelope her in his arms, but once he saw her, he couldn't bring himself to disturb her. She was the epitome of satisfaction.

He had to face it. He wasn't nineteen anymore—he was nearly thirty-one—but she'd awakened a power in him that hadn't surged in a decade, spurring a series of encores in the bedroom. He'd made love to her three times last night, including once on the kitchen floor, and he would've done it again had she not fallen asleep on his chest a few hours ago.

Now in restless slumber, she smelled of sex and raspberry-vanilla. And probably tasted even sweeter. One of her hands was lost in a halo of curls at her head; the other rested just below her navel.

He crawled out of bed and reached for the sketchpad and pencils under it. Instead, he pulled out a note: *Top shelf in the closet.* It figured.

Once he found his supplies, he positioned himself beneath the window. When he turned back to her, a tingling surge ran up his spine and left him breathless.

The position of her hand at her abdomen suddenly struck him as the picture of an expectant mother, waiting to feel the first flutters of life within her. He managed to exhale again and pressed the pencil to paper.

Lines of charcoal became a mass of unruly hair. Swoops became

81

the curve of a hip, a breast.

"Hmmm."

His subject's eyes flickered open. She shifted position, lifted her hand from its precious cradle upon her stomach, and blinked.

"Hi." He rolled the pencil between his fingers, bracing himself for her reaction. Would she be angry he was drawing her without permission? She yawned, closed her eyes, and returned to her previous position. A small smile appeared on her lips, but she was quick to contain it. "Carry on, bright eyes." She wanted him to finish the drawing. Quite possibly, it was the best gift he'd ever received.

"Thanks." His charcoal flew over the paper, blending with the fingers on his left hand, sketching with his right. Smearing, stroking, thumbing, patting. He reached for a pastel crayon.

He mixed the charcoal with the lightest pink pastel, highlighting where the rays of the rising sun fell onto her beautiful body. He filtered a deep rose throughout the twisted bedclothes, boasting of the passion she had set aflame there.

Another urge crept into his creative mind, and he flipped to a blank slate. This time, he zeroed in on her mouth, on the lips that had been torturing and consuming him.

He'd kissed them exhaustively, and they looked like it, too. Rosy, swollen, tender, alive. And recorded forever on paper, like a last will and testament.

Desire built between his legs, but he toiled on. There was still more of her to capture.

He flipped again and sketched the hollow of her throat, the divot in her chin, her long, thick lashes. Her inner wrists, her bare wedding ring finger, the freckle on the left cheek of her backside. Damn, finding that little treasure had been a treat.

He drew her breasts, he drew her ankles, he drew the softest part of her thigh, the part he wanted desperately to kiss. Then again, he wanted to kiss all her parts, from the crown of her head to the bottoms of her feet.

Unable to catch his breath, he tossed his pencil aside and crawled into bed.

"Done?"

He shook his head but didn't speak. No, he wasn't done. He didn't know if he ever would be. With a pastel-stained index, he traced her lips and stared down at her.

*   *   *

She knew what he wanted. He was nude, hard, and leaning over her. His eyes shone with an animal desire, begging her to sate him, and he dragged his finger from her mouth to her cheek.

Never breaking eye contact, she touched him in prelude, caressing the length of him in her palm. He trembled and a forlorn hesitation appeared in his eyes, as if he didn't believe he deserved the pleasure. He seemed uncertain, vulnerable, and so different from the confident man to whom she'd grown accustomed.

There was no question she was going to offer what he wanted. This was about giving, evidence of her dedication, and she'd share in the pleasure she'd provide him. He traced her lips with his thumb, and she parted them, intending to reassure him. But he closed his eyes and drew in a long breath before she said a word.

She lured him in closer, maneuvered him onto his back with gentle pressure to his chest, and trailed a finger along the perfect diamond concave nestled between his pecs and upper abs. He shuddered when she breathed a kiss there.

Unsure fingers raked against her neck and into her hair. She swept a garland of kisses down his chest, over his stomach, palming him all the while, tickling his testicles with her fingertips, and giving them a gentle tug.

Eager to taste him, she turned her lips toward him, breathing against his hot skin, dragging her tongue along the length of him. One hand tensed in her hair; the other brushed along the contour of her cheek. She worked her mouth over his engorged flesh, massaging him inch by inch, deeper and deeper, until she'd engulfed him, flexing her tongue against the underside of his shaft.

He gasped, and she reached up to feel his muscled chest, evidence of hard, physical labor, which tightened with every stroke of her tongue. A strong heartbeat reverberated beneath her fingers. At that moment, she felt as vital to his survival as the blood coursing through his veins. For once, he needed her. His fingers trailed from her cheek, along her neck, over her shoulder, threading a path up her arm and meeting her hand on his chest with a gentle squeeze. Every muscle in his body tensed against her, and the slightest quiver ran through the length of him. He squeezed her hand with more intensity, and large fingers went rigid in her hair.

"Nicki," he breathed. A split second later, he withdrew from her mouth, and two strong arms pulled her from his lap and snuggled her against his warm chest. She placed a hand over his heart, and he pressed a kiss at the crown of her head.

"Give me a minute," he said. "I almost came."

She felt her brow furrow. *Well, wasn't that was the intent?*

"I want you to feel good, too." He brushed hair from her forehead. "And trust me. You're going to."

When she turned in his embrace to meet his gaze, a dull ache settled into her muscles, a reminder of the preceding hours of lovemaking. Scorching. Passionate. Yet woven with an element of respect she'd never before experienced.

He looked down at her, his fingers lacing through her hair, massaging her scalp. Blue eyes zinged right into her heart, inspiring a rush of heat between her thighs. He was everything she'd always imagined him to be—attentive, patient, thorough—and the one thing she'd never dared to dream: hers.

*   *   *

At seven in the morning, with framers straggling in half an hour late, Ty stapled a sketch to the studs in the master bathroom. "Changes." He nodded at two men. "And we're short on time."

"Behind schedule, not even under roof, and we're remodeling," one of them said.

"That's right," Ty said. "Remodeling on the go."

"Orders from Pussy Galore?"

"Orders from your foreman and boss—me." Ty set his jaw, but the punk didn't flinch. "It's what superior custom homebuilders do, when they see a way to better the project, and they do it without complaining. Get to work."

One of the men leaned against a stud and puffed a leisurely drag off a cigarette.

"If we're not framed in three weeks' time," Ty said, "we're behind schedule on the next frame, too, and it's hard enough to make up time on one house, let alone two."

"Can't handle two houses? You're handling two women," the punk said. "Granted, not very well. You knocked one up, and the other's making changes on your job site."

Ty silently counted to ten and shifted his Three-peat cap. "Don't believe everything you hear. Changes aside, there's no reason for you not to have your ass working already, other than god-damned laziness. Get on it."

When he turned away, he met with Montalvo's shoulder. The

84

journeyman shoved past him.

"I need you downstairs, Montalvo."

No response.

"Rework the butler's pass. Before noon."

Montalvo gave half a nod. "Yes, ma'am."

Ty pinched the bridge of his nose and headed toward the stairs. So much for personal progress with the journeyman.

*   *   *

Nicki stared at her cell phone. Her mother had yet to return her call. Fort Lauderdale was a new beginning in more ways than one. She looked across the bistro table in the garden and watched Verna twist her dark hair into a clip. The Isle of Venice was her home now, and the woman opposite her was the closest she'd find to a mother figure.

"Where's the closest place to shop?" Nicki brought a ripe strawberry, a small morsel of Verna's proffered brunch, to her lips.

"Well that all depends on what it is you're shopping for," Verna said. "You come to the right place, here at number twenty-five, if you're in the market for a great f—"

"Verna!"

The older woman winked. "Not that I know from personal experience, you understand, but with a body like that, I'll bet he ain't nothing but great in the sack. Arms like a rock-n-roll drummer, ready to take you down, and mmm-mmm, good." With her teeth, she yanked the cork from last night's bottle of champagne. "You drinking orange juice with your bubbly this morning?"

With a conscious decision to keep her jaw from hitting the ground, Nicki shook her head. "Just orange juice, thanks."

"Shoot, I'm gonna be drunk by noon if I have to swallow the rest of this by my lonesome. You sure?"

"Quite."

Verna shrugged and splashed some champagne into her juice. "So what you looking to buy?"

"Work boots."

"Shops along Las Olas might be too swanky and boutique-like for something so rough and tumble, though it's just a few blocks away. Costume jewelry, home accessorizing stores, art galleries—"

Nicki dropped her strawberry onto her plate and looked up.

Verna gulped her morning drink. "Photography studios, sculptures…you name it. But you won't find a boot on the boulevard made for anything more than strutting your stuff, I guarantee. Though you do have stuff to strut, that's for sure. You always been this curvy?"

"Obviously not." Not that Ty had noticed, anyway.

"Now don't be shy, gingerbread. Have some more." She sprinkled a few berries onto Nicki's plate.

*   *   *

An hour later, leaving Verna to bake in the hot sun, Nicki wandered down a red brick sidewalk, a quiet observer on Las Olas Boulevard. Women of high couture clicked past with handled shopping bags, checking their watches, following agendas. Students occupied outdoor café tables, sketching on pads, sharing lattés.

Too intrigued to stop, she pressed on, eager for what she'd find on the next block. If Fort Lauderdale was home, Las Olas was her kitchen. Cozy, comfortable. Where she belonged.

When she'd walked nearly a mile, she met with a scurry at the intersection of Southeast 2nd Court. She peered down the street and a two-story, white building with arched windows caught her eye: Las Olas Art Center. She couldn't refuse the temptation.

She entered the wide, spacious gallery, scanning a board of announcements: Dr. Toby Levinson's Art History Forum. Coming Soon to the Everglades Exhibit Room: The Watercolors of Resident Artist Clay McClelland. Models wanted for Ann Worth's "Chocolate Sea," inquire... *Model wanted?* She looked more closely. Inquire upstairs. Dare she?

She walked further into the building, and a clay sculpture instantly caught her eye. It was the shape of a woman's back, but without the allure of breasts on the opposite side. Sexy. Riveting. The curve of a shoulder, the line of a spine. A gorgeous woman must have sat for the artist; envy coursed through her. She fought the urge to trace the contour of the piece with her fingers. She'd never be that..."Beautiful."

"Thanks."

"Is this you?" Nicki asked over her shoulder of a woman—mid-thirties, Nicki guessed—clad in a black leather bustier and a long, swishing skirt as blazing orange as the hair framing her face.

"No, it's mine. My work. Hardly a self portrait." She blew an orange spike of hair out of her eyes. "Annie. Resident artist."

No posing. Ty's words rang in her ears like cathedral bells breaking through a thunderstorm. *No posing, no posing, no posing.* She extended her hand. "Nicki. I'm a model."

86

*   *   *

The day had been less productive than Ty had hoped, but he was glad when the last crew members sauntered out the door nearly an hour early at three o'clock. It had been a grueling day, but Nicki waiting at home for him gave him something to look forward to.

While he straightened the site in preparation to leave, stacking two-by-fours, sweeping floors, a familiar soprano floated up from the ground level. "I just need a minute, Ty."

Mandy. He propped a hand against a stud and swiped a bicep over his sweaty forehead. Her heels clicked against the stairs. "Don't come up. I'll be right there."

"I don't mind—"

"Stay there." He dropped the broom and headed toward her, a perspiring, dirty mess clambering down shaky stairs.

She wore a white cotton shirt, the bottom three buttons unfastened. If he didn't know she was pregnant, he probably wouldn't have noticed the small baby bubble peeking up from her low-rise capri pants, but he couldn't take his eyes from it now. His or not, a tiny life was forming in there.

"Hi," he said, rubbing his hands together.

She didn't smile, but tossed her head, jostling the chestnut hair hanging in her eyes. "I miss you."

"This isn't about me." He walked around her, nodding at her tummy and making his way toward his portable workbench. "It's about that little girl. Nothing else."

"How can it not be about you? I left my whole life behind when things ended between us. My job, our friends—"

"No friend of mine would take my girl to bed."

"I know I hurt you, but you have to believe me. Nothing happened that morning."

He rolled the blueprints and pulled a rubber band from his pocket. Maybe Nicki would start planning furniture layouts this week. On the way home, he'd make copies of the plans for her. "What did Shakespeare say about protesting too much?" He wound the band around the plans.

"Nothing happened. And I'm going to say it until you believe me."

"Save your breath."

She grabbed his hand.

"I'm dirty."

"I don't care." She forced his palm against her womb. "No matter what you say, this is about you and me."

He licked sweat from his upper lip and slid his hand from her grasp. "I have to get going."

"Ty—"

"I have a lot to do at home."

"If this baby isn't yours, prove it to me."

"What's to prove?" Heat crawled into his cheeks, but he immediately regained his composure, and swallowed his anger. "There's nothing to prove, Mandy."

He led her out of the home-in-progress, opened the door of her SUV, and closed the door behind her.

She started the car and stared at him through the open window. "I'll be back, you know."

"Just…concentrate on taking care of your baby."

"Our baby."

"That baby's not mine, and we both know it. If I submit a sample for testing, will you admit it?"

"If you agree to test, it'll only prove it's yours."

"Fine. I consent to testing, and I'll provide a sample as soon as my lawyer can arrange it."

*   *   *

Imagine—casting human body parts in chocolate. It was an interesting project, to say the least. Nicki flipped through Annie's sketches of hands, feet, breasts, penises in various erectile stages…"The exhibit's in September?"

The artist nodded. "I'll be starting construction at the beginning of August."

It figured. August. Just when her real work with Ty would begin. But still, how much furniture could a girl buy in a day? And if she began working on schemes now, she might have extra time. "How many hours would you need me?"

"Total? I don't know. I'd like to use your feet, your belly. Definitely your bosom. Thirty, maybe forty hours tops. And two hours Tuesday and Thursday afternoons, starting now, if you're interested."

"Tuesday and Thursday?"

"I teach a class at Broward Community College. It's hard to get a model at ten dollars an hour, four hours a week, smack dab in the middle of the day."

"What kind of class? Sculpture?"

Annie shook her head. "Drawing 201."

"My rate is fifteen." Where the hell had that come from? The Art Institute hadn't paid her as much, and here she would've posed for free, for the opportunity to be part of Annie's Chocolate Sea of body parts. She was about to recant her counter-offer when—

"For that, you're bound 'til the end of the term, okay? Tuesdays and Thursdays, two o'clock. Las Olas campus. Now until May, with an option to extend through my summer session."

"I can handle that." *But could Ty?* Posing for a woman was different than posing for a man, and he might accept the Chocolate Sea. But sitting for a class was another matter. Perhaps if she explained that the class came hand-in-hand with the most intriguing exhibit she'd ever taken part in, he'd understand.

"Bring your own robe," Annie said.

"Will do."

Nicki made her way back to the Isle of Venice, a battle of morals exploding in her mind.

I'm a model. This is what I do.

It's something Ty has never approved of.

Only because he doesn't understand.

Regardless, it's a betrayal.

Maybe what he doesn't know won't hurt him.

It was with that thought she found Ty hanging his head on the front porch, looking more than damaged. Guilt fluttered through her. While she knew she wasn't responsible for his defeat today, she might be, should he learn of her recent dealings at Las Olas Art Center.

"Hey, bright eyes."

He looked up, a natural smile illuminating his eyes. "Hey, Nicki. Where you been?"

"You know…wandering. How was your day?"

One corner of his mouth twitched. "Come here."

"That good, huh?" When she stopped at the top of the porch stairs, he pulled her into his lap, his rugged hands roaming up her back in a thorough exploration.

He kissed her on the mouth with open, inviting lips. "It's about to get a hell of a lot better." His voice was gruff. "That's for damn sure."

CHAPTER 9

"Will you relax?" Montalvo rolled a tape measure along the longest wall in the master bedroom. A hot, teasing breeze filtered up from the Atlantic.

Late May in south Florida felt like Chicago's mid-July. Ty crossed his arms over his bare chest, gnawing on his bottom lip. "Her furniture layout's tight as it is, and I don't want that sitting area to look cramped. What do we have?"

"For the love of God, it doesn't matter if we're an inch or two off," came a comment from the group of framers taking a break on the level below. "What are you going to do if we are? Rework it all?"

Ty ignored the snickers that followed. "What's the dimension?"

"What do we need?" Montalvo didn't take his eyes from the tape.

"Twenty-four, nine. Bare minimum."

"We're twenty four, ten-and-a-half. We're fine."

At last Ty breathed. "Let's go over where we marked plumbing centers again. Cabinets are on order, and—"

Montalvo clipped the tape measure at his hip. "No."

"What?"

The journeyman cracked a knuckle. "Carmichael, we been over this whole place. There's never been a rough frame so on spec, and the foundation can't settle fast enough to change the dimensions from yesterday. Face it—we're done."

Ty shifted his Three-peat cap.

"I'd think you'd be happy to be rid of us," Montalvo said. "Ship us off to West Palm Beach to work on the next frame, and go sit behind some desk, pushing pencils, where you belong. Leave the real man's work to us."

"Never been a rough frame built so close to spec, and you think I'm going to quit?"

"You got lucky. Good crew."

"Lucky? I got a genius of a journeyman, but four of the laziest sons-of-bitches I've ever seen working under him. The only thing lucky about this job is that we've finished only two weeks behind schedule."

"You know what else you got?" The journeyman grinned. "Company."

"Carmichael," Ray Diamond called from below. "Got a minute?"

No, he didn't have a minute. Between the wrap on this frame, walk-throughs with plumbers and electricians, and the new framing in West Palm Beach, he didn't have time to breathe, but he made his way down the stairs. As soon as his foot touched the first-floor deck, his boss shoved a large manila envelope into his hands.

"Have a look," Ray said.

Under the scrutiny of his crew, Ty opened the envelope and pulled out several matted perspectives of the kitchen, great room, library… Nicki's work.

"Care to explain?" Ray fixed him with a hard stare.

"Concept boards."

"And?"

"And what? It's what I plan to do with the place. Thought you might like to see what I'm doing with the decorating budget."

"And I thought you'd like to see this." Ray slapped the Broward County Building Commissioner's letterhead atop the concept boards.

"What is it?" Ty glanced up at his boss, who sported a smile a mile wide.

"Read it."

Mr. Diamond, upon study of your architectural plans and further conceptual drawings, I am pleased to announce your qualification for Key Status in the category of custom homes greater than four-thousand square feet…

"We beat out Bertolli," Ty said. He looked up from the paper to see the crew gathering close. "We won the Key."

Ray nodded. "Damn right we did."

*   *   *

Nicki rushed from Annie's classroom and glanced at the clock on her cell phone. Ten after four. If she ran, she might make it to the Isle of Venice before Ty arrived home. And still no call from her mother.

No contact with her family, and since she'd arrived, none of the Carmichaels had called either. She and Ty floated like an island in south Florida, as if Chicago were an illusion, but the Second City loomed in her mind, a formidable, constant presence. It was there that Ty and Robert Carmichael had butted heads over the most mundane— as well as major—occurrences in the family's design firm. And in Chicago, Nicki had been orphaned. Not only when her faceless father left months before her birth, but again four years ago, when Jeanine married. What was it with parents who refused to acknowledge their children?

With confidence brewing fresh from her recent studio session, she stepped onto Las Olas Boulevard and dialed.

The recorded voice of her mother's husband sounded tinny through the receiver. "You have reached Carl, Jeanine, Charlie, and Jake. We can't come to the phone now, but—"

No use in leaving another message when Jeanine had neglected answer the four she'd left already. She was about to hang up when she heard, "Nicki?"

She put the phone back to her ear. "Mom?"

"Nicki, I thought that was your cell number. I've been meaning to call you, but you have no idea how busy we've been."

"That's all right."

"But you know naptime's almost over, so I gotta run."

"Can't you talk for—"

"God, where are you? I can hardly hear you. Let's get together next week for lunch, okay? I'll make it up to you."

"Next week? Mom, I'm in—"

"Or the week after, whatever works. Gotta run. Bye."

Nicki closed her phone and inhaled the heavy air. She stopped in her tracks and breathed in the sultry scents surrounding her—pavement, coconut oil, buttery garlic wafting from a nearby restaurant. The hot breeze caressed her skin. Ty would be home when she got there. He'd comfort her through her mother's insurmountable and repeated rejection.

It was no wonder she'd run to Ty when she'd lost control in Chicago. He'd proven he cared for her time and again, when no one else had paid attention. And how had she repaid him? She caught sight of a poster in the window of La Casa De Mario. *Student Exhibit. August 1-7. Las Olas Art Center. All amateur works welcome.* She'd been posing behind his back.

*   *   *

Ty's first instinct had been to rush home to Nicki to celebrate winning the Key Award, but a strange thing happened before he'd set foot off the job site. The snottiest punk on the crew had shaken his hand.

Now, at an outdoor beer garden along Route A1A, Ty excused himself when the group ordered a second pitcher. He couldn't afford even the slightest hangover tomorrow, with the onset of double duty between the Key House and the new frame in West Palm Beach.

Besides, the Key Award was a great accomplishment, but National Finals for Custom Homebuilder of the Year seemed as untouchable as peace of mind, despite the small victory under his belt.

Across A1A, at a beachside stand, he could see Mandy lick at a generous scoop of chocolate gelato. It was her favorite place for the treat, and he'd taken her there many times. Good to know she'd found someone else to accompany her—Tabor.

Ty hurried down the promenade, hoping to remain invisible. He couldn't help glancing every now and then at the swell of her belly, which she proudly displayed in a snug halter top. After a quick calculation, he figured her to be about five-and-a-half months along, and she barely looked it. Strangers probably thought she was simply chunky around the middle, but he knew the truth.

The truth. Although he'd submitted a DNA sample, Mandy had refused to take the next step. The baby's DNA could be gathered before birth through an amnio-something, but Mandy had yet to comply.

And there she was, laughing, and hanging on Tabor's arm. He quickened his pace across the street where he'd parked, and slid behind the wheel. *Start on the first turn, Betty. Come on, girl. Cooperate.* He turned the key and the engine's murmur rumbled into a hum. *Thank you.*

He sped down Las Olas Boulevard, over New River Sound, and hooked the car onto Isle of Venice Drive. The open front door at number twenty-five meant Nicki was home. She preferred fresh air, however heavy and hot, to air conditioning. He wouldn't argue the subject tonight. This evening they'd celebrate the notch in his tool belt: the Key.

"Nicki?" His voice echoed throughout the first floor, getting no response. He shoved off his work boots and pattered to the kitchen to drop his keys in their designated basket. "I'm home, kid."

A thud from above answered him. He rushed toward the sound and found her in a spare bedroom, flushed with heat in cut-offs and a tank top. The oppressive breeze puffing through the open window provided little relief from the heat. She'd piled her hair under a ratty, red bandana, but stray tendrils stuck to her moist cheeks. His old drill was firmly in her grasp, and drywall screws poked from between her luscious, pink lips. Sheetrock covered most of the bottom half of the far wall.

"What are you doing?"

She plucked a screw from her mouth and drilled it into a four-by-eight piece of sheetrock, with only a glance in his direction. Her eyes were tired and red.

"Nicki?"

"What does it look like I'm doing?" The remaining screw bounced as she spoke.

"Drywall."

"There you have it then." She shrugged, positioned the remaining screw, and drilled it into the stud.

"But why?"

"Because I can't live like this, I can't take it anymore, and if you're too busy to finish a damn project, I'll do it myself."

"When you drywall, you leave half an inch at the bottom."

"You might. I don't."

"That's how it's done, kid."

"Stop calling me that." She yanked the cord from the outlet, wound it around the drill, and dropped it into its faded box.

Where she had found that box? He hadn't seen it since…he didn't know when. "I have great news."

"I need a shower."

"Give me a minute."

"No." She shouldered past him, removing her soaked tank top as she walked. It wasn't until she exhaled a long, dramatic sigh that he recognized the catch in her breath. It sounded as if she were about to—

He caught her elbow and spun her sweating body into his arms. "You're crying."

"No, I'm not." With that, she buried her head in his chest.

"I know this place drives you nuts, sweetheart." He drummed his fingers against the small of her back. Although her bruises had healed, the picture of her black-and-blue flesh remained with him, a constant reminder of how fragile a strong woman could be, when in the hands of an undeserving man.

"I'm fine." She met his gaze and slipped out of his arms. "I need a shower."

He followed her down the hallway, through his bedroom, and leaned against the bathroom doorframe, his heart reverberating with impending doom. There was only one reason she'd choose to work on a bedroom: space of her own. "Why a bedroom?"

"What?" She started the shower, returned to the vanity, and slinked out of her shorts.

Great panties—triple string bikini. Black satin. Gorgeous, enticing curves. "The entire house is in pieces. Why a bedroom?"

She shrugged. "I talked to Mom today." At last she looked at him. "She didn't even know I wasn't in Chicago anymore."

He exhaled in relief. "Come here."

"I'm fine, Ty. I just—"

"Come here."

"I'm a mess."

"So am I." He strode to her, pulled her clammy body into his arms, the sweat of their bodies melding, mixing. "She's a selfish woman who doesn't know a damn thing about what's important. Don't let her get to you."

She licked her lips. "You're good to me, you know that? I don't deserve this."

"You're right. You deserve so much more."

Her lips brushed against his bicep, and his muscle tightened at the intimate caress.

*   *   *

She didn't deserve any of it. Not the arms around her, not his kind words. He'd asked one thing of her—to stay out of studios—and she'd been posing since shortly after she'd arrived. Furthermore, she'd allowed him to believe her mother was responsible for her mood, in lieu of a guilty conscience. *Come clean.* "Ty, I..."

His hands wandered into her hair, and he pulled off the sweat-drenched bandana. "Nice work on the concept boards, by the way."

Tell him. She swallowed hard. "It was nothing. And you've already thanked me."

"Not enough." A thick finger lifted her chin, forcing her to look at him.

Such a beautiful man. Inside and out.

He twitched a smile. "We got it, Nicki. We won the Key."

"Oh, Ty. That's—"

He kissed her and carried her into the tub. An energetic stream of lukewarm water washed away the day's dirt and sweat—and the words she had yet to confess.

CHAPTER 10

The sound of the shower awakened Nicki at a quarter after seven. Why hadn't Ty left for the job site yet? She leaned up on her elbows. Crisp cotton sheets caressed her nude body, and, through the open window, she stared at distant palms, swaying in the serene August breeze. She'd been in Fort Lauderdale for four months, and the tranquility of the city never ceased to amaze her.

Rarely did she ponder her life in Chicago, except to acknowledge it was over. The man she'd agreed to marry had phoned a few times, but when she'd neglected to return the calls, he'd disappeared like a bad dream. Her mother seemed equally as invisible, but didn't leave a void either, and as long as her roommate received Nicki's scraped-together portion of the rent check every month—thank goodness for Annie and the posing gigs at the art center—her roommate had no complaints.

She took in a lungful of intracoastal breeze, savoring the salt and loam scent, as if it were the product of a five-star restaurant. *Feels like, sounds like, smells like, looks like, tastes like home.*

If the windows in this room became French doors, Ty could build a veranda above the garden—a private morning haven, where they could breakfast on Sunday mornings. He'd probably draw her on that terrace, make love to her at dusk among the scent of the wildflowers growing below. Maybe he'd ask her to stay forever.

Stay. The very word made her heart flip.

The sound of his singing filtered through the door. He never sang outside of the shower, and he always sang the same song in there.

His baritone singing the old Eagles' tune grew like a crescendo when she opened the door and stepped into the steamy bathroom. She brushed her teeth.

His voice was crisp and on key, never faltering. Either he didn't know she'd entered, or audiences didn't scare him. She stepped into the tub behind him.

Nothing but sinew and strength, his deltoid muscles flexed as he ran his hands through his hair and chased suds away. Unable to deny herself the pleasure, she slipped her arms around his waist, pressing her tender breasts against his back.

He didn't flinch, simply sang about highways and signs, squeezed her hand, and reached for her bottle of body wash.

The raspberry-vanilla scent of her soap filled the room, and he turned toward her with a smile. "'Morning, kid." He smeared pink suds over her shoulders, breasts, and hips, deposited her beneath the stream of water, and encircled her body with his arms. "How did you sleep?"

"I don't remember sleeping very much. You?"

"I took an elbow to the ribs."

"Did not. And happy birthday!"

"I did so. You're vicious."

"Sorry."

"Feel like shopping today?"

"When?" She had a ten o'clock slot with Annie. Today they'd mold her breasts for the September chocolate exhibit.

"What do you mean, when? Whenever."

"What about work?"

"I've put in five months of sixty-hour weeks. You know that."

"I also know winning the Key Award was worth it. But you aren't stopping at the Key, remember?"

"True, I'm not Custom Homebuilder of the Year, but I'm taking the day off, and I want to spend it with you."

"I'd love to. But I have…plans."

"Plans? Doing what?"

After a deep breath, during which she considered and denied the urge to tell him about the Chocolate Sea, she shrugged. "I'm going to hit a shop on Las Olas for your gift. Give me until noon?"

"You're gift enough, but sure. I thought we'd take a water taxi toward the Galleria."

She'd seen water taxis along the intracoastal, but she'd yet to ride on one. "Whatever you want."

"Oh, I think you've taken care of what I want." He brushed a soapy finger over her chin. He scrunched her hair, and his lips met hers. "Make it quick on Las Olas, will you?"

*   *   *

A heavy knock sounded over the clank of terra cotta tile meeting the floor. Ty looked up from the diagonal pattern and peered down the hallway, sweat dripping from beneath his backwards hat, despite the central air blasting throughout the house. "Yeah?"

The doorknob twisted and Mandy peeked in. "Busy?"

Ty swallowed hard and looked at his bare wrist; he'd forgotten his watch. *How long until Nicki comes back?* He cleared his throat. "What time is it?"

"Around ten."

"I only have a minute."

"That's all I need." She emerged, wearing a pink-and-white striped sundress, her belly round, attractive, and not nearly as large as he expected it to be. "I went to your site first, but no one's there."

"I'm waiting for the trim crew to finish up a few things." He stood. "But as for my part, I'm about done."

"It's looking good over there. Heard you won the Key."

"What can I do for you?"

"Happy birthday." She paused at the powder room door, lifted a finger to the square, leaded glass insert that always reminded him of the window in a wine cellar door. Nicki had called it mission style with a country French influence. He took her word for it. "I like the new door."

"Thanks." He shifted his weight from one foot to the other. "How's Tabor?"

"I didn't come to talk about him."

"I can't imagine we have much else to discuss, Mandy."

"I'm dilated to three."

"What does that mean?"

"It's a stage of labor."

"It's early yet." Almost a month early, and if she delivered now, that would mean—

"I thought you should know."

"Oh." He rubbed his hands together and stared at her, searching deep within his soul for a connection, a feeling, anything. But there was nothing there, despite the possibility of an early delivery. "Thanks for letting me know." He brushed past her and opened the door. "'Bye."

*   *   *

Unclothed from the waist up, Nicki lay on a collapsible table, staring at the ceiling while Annie worked papier maché strips around her nipples.

Her body, her form, was all over the student exhibit in the first floor gallery. Several students had banded together to display her from several angles. Good thing Ty was too busy to attend a showcase. But what would she do if he happened upon some random rendering?

He knew her body better than anyone. Knew just how to touch her, just how to kiss and caress her. He could draw her with his eyes closed, and he sure as hell would recognize her figure on paper.

If she felt strongly about posing, why was she hiding the fact she was doing it? And if he really cared for her, wouldn't he accept her passion?

That's it. You're telling him today.

*   *   *

That baby wasn't his. But he didn't know enough about pregnancy to formulate an argument, should Nicki not believe him when he told her. And he couldn't put off telling her any longer. *Nicki, my ex-girlfriend is pregnant. She thinks I'm the father, but I'm not. And this is how I know for sure...*

Dressed casually, he made his way down the street to number thirty-one, knocked on the door, and entered the foyer, cluttered with the same boxes marked "George's crap" that had always been there. The usual aroma of lavender incense greeted him. "Verna?"

The faded blue linoleum in the hallway was mottled with fresh splatters of bright yellow paint, and he followed the dribbles to the sunroom, where Verna was painting over faded wallpaper with a four-inch paint brush. She'd pulled the weathered rattan furniture, piled with the deceased's old sport coats and boxes, a few inches from the wall and appeared to be painting around it.

"'Morning, Verna."

She turned to him and grinned, purple gum snapping between her teeth. "Hey, sugar plum, happy birthday."

"Thanks. What are you doing?"

"That son-of-a-bitch just won't quit." She whisked a tendril of black hair from her eyes, streaking it the color of cartoon sunshine. "Every

100

damn morning he's here, staring at me, accusing me of living my life without him."

"Verna—"

She looked toward the ground. "I got news for you, Georgie Porgie. You lived your life plenty without me, so I'm hiking my skirts up now you're gone."

"What happened now?"

"I think he's planning on spending the sweet here-after right in my sunroom. And if that's what he wants to do, I suppose I can't stop him. His name's still on the deed, after all, but I can sure as glitz make it hard on him. He always hated yellow." Again, she addressed the demons in hell. "Didn't you, you skank-chasing slug? Well, I got you now, don't I?"

Ty slipped his hands into his pants pockets and kicked aside an orange ball of yarn that lay near his feet. "Are you all right?"

"Never been better."

"Stop painting, Verna. Nicki and I can help you with this later. I'll strip the wallpaper, paint the whole wall—and with a roller."

Verna clucked her tongue. "Whoa, that Nicki of yours. Sweet as a Key lime. If I were a man—or maybe a lesbian, it don't matter which—I'd sure like to know what makes her sing."

"Well, don't change your orientation. I can answer that for you."

"Bet you can. You tell her yet? About that baby?"

"It isn't mine."

"Might be. You tell her?"

"I'm trying to. I'm going to."

She stared at him with a gaping mouth and released the paint brush.

He watched it sink into the gallon of paint. "I know, Verna. I know I should've told her already, but—"

"What in the devil's incarnation are you waiting for?"

"I don't want to hurt her, and—"

"Gumdrop, you're hurting her more by keeping it from her. Are you hoping that damn secretary's going to withdraw the lawsuit? That some iron-clad knight is going to fly in on a horse named Trigger and stake claim to that child? Ain't never going to happen, and that hair-brain from Hendricks ain't no nearer a sire than my dead husband. You tell Nicki, or she'll hear tell from someone else." Her gum cracked and popped. "This city ain't as booming a metropolis as your precious Chi-town, and you're far from anonymous on this here isle."

Ty nodded in silence, his gut churning.

"That Tabor is dying to get you on something, and heavens to Francine, this just might be it."

"Verna, you're a woman."

"Last I checked I had all the equipment to make me so. Ain't used it in a few days, but..." She shrugged. "I'm getting up there in years, suppose it's to be expected."

"If you're pregnant, what does it mean if you're dilated to three?"

"How would I know?"

"Verna, you have five daughters."

"Sure I do, but—"

"And you have eight grandchildren."

"Yep. But back in my day, you was pregnant if a rabbit died. And then some time later, you had a baby. Sometimes while conscious, but sometimes not. We didn't hear about this such-and-such dilation, and for all that made the grass grow, we sure didn't read about it. I don't know diddly about pregnancy in this day and age." She stared into the paint can, dipping a finger just below the surface. "Well, shoot me in the breast. You got me so distracted I lost my paintbrush."

"Leave it in there," Ty said before she submerged her entire hand. "I'll finish up in here later this week."

"Later in the week, huh? I suppose it can't hurt to live with him a few more days." She clenched her fists and looked down again. "But so help me, George, if I catch you doing my crosswords—"

"I have to go," Ty said. "I'm taking Nicki shopping."

Verna smiled, batting her fake lashes. "You tell her about that baby, okay? Don't let this get any more out of hand than it is already."

He knew Verna was right. Despite her wacky tendencies, she was always right, but without the information he needed, how was he supposed to tell Nicki? Maybe his mother would be able to fill him in. Maybe he could conjure up the courage to call her before he took Nicki out.

Or maybe she'd call him. It *was* his birthday after all. A nice thought, but he wouldn't hear from his parents today. Freddi might call. Maybe Krissy would, too, if she could pull herself out of Claude-Phillipe's arms for a moment. He froze outside his front door, homesick for the first time. He'd abandoned all of them the day he left, and if Nicki hadn't blown into town like a breath of fresh air to remind him from where he'd hailed, he might have forgotten.

He heard her talking inside, probably on the telephone. For a moment, his heart tightened in anticipation. Had she fielded a call from his family?

"I expect him back in a few minutes." Nicki's voice was coming from the kitchen. "Are you sure I can't take a message?"

Dread replaced anticipation when he realized any number of women could be on the other end of that line, and one in particular worried him. He entered and hurried down the hallway. "I'll let him know you called. Thank you." She hung up the phone just as he crossed the threshold.

"Any chance that was my mother?"

"No." Her smile relieved him, and the sight of her in an angelic, white satin robe was cause enough to cancel the water taxi. "But Ms. Washington would like you to call, when you have a minute."

The blood drained from his face, he was sure of it, and his lungs felt as if they weighed over one hundred pounds. "What did she want?"

"I didn't ask."

"Why did you answer it?"

She brushed past him with a smile, speaking over her shoulder on her way up the stairs. "Am I something worth hiding?"

Just the opposite actually. It isn't you I'm concealing. "Come on, Nicki. I didn't mean it that way."

"Call her back, bright eyes," she said from the stairs. "I told her you would."

He sighed and chased the scent of her up the stairs. "I didn't mean…" The aromatic mixture of her skin and lingerie consumed him when he reached her. His head spun and the general between his legs saluted. "God."

"You don't have to explain." She disappeared into the closet.

"Yes, I do."

"What's to explain? For a brief moment in time, you wanted to marry someone. So did I. Things fall apart, right?"

Raspberries and roses carried him into the closet, and he took her half-naked body into his arms, cradling her curls. She really was the greatest. So young, but confident. What other woman in his sexual history book would treat an ex-lover's phone call with such indifference?

"I'm sorry." He tightened his arms around her, unwilling to release her. "I guess I'm a little keyed up, knowing my family won't call."

"You could reach out, too, you know. Take the first step."

"They should call first." He shook his head. "There's something to be said about parental responsibility." How ironic that those words would bounce off his tongue amid the mess with Mandy. He was hardly willing to step up to the plate in that department, assuming the responsibility was his to claim. Which it wasn't.

She brushed her lips against his. "When I'm a parent, there's no way anything will come between my children and me. I'll always take the higher ground, no matter how low it makes me feel. But point blank, some people aren't cut from that cloth. My mother isn't, and your father isn't either."

"Do you..." He licked his lips, imagining he could taste her kiss. "Do you think about children? Having them?"

"Sure. Sometimes."

"I do, too. A lot lately."

A smile touched her lips. "Charming."

"But scary, too. Babies change things. Everything, actually. I'd like a house full someday," he said, deciding so that very second. "Eight or nine."

She pressed her fists against his chest, laughing. "Then let me save you a lot of time and trouble. I'm the wrong candidate for that job. Most women are, as a matter of fact."

"All right, three." He caught her lovely, square chin in his hand. "Maybe four."

"How about one at a time, at the right time?"

He kissed her full on the mouth, and suddenly, the right time seemed to be just around the corner.

CHAPTER 11

Ty boarded the banana yellow water taxi, complete with a blue-and-yellow striped canopy, and with true chivalry, he held out a hand to help her aboard. "Galleria," he told the taxi captain.

Although the water taxi sat at least six, they were the only two aboard. She sank onto a yellow cushioned bench. The fresh air gently fingered through her hair, and Ty's massive right hand came to rest upon her thigh.

"I can tell you anything, right?" he asked.

"It's occasionally been my experience that I can't shut you up."

"Good, because I have a confession to make," he said. He touched a curl at her temple with his ring finger. "And it requires an open mind."

The frightening, serious look in his eyes silenced her, caused a gallop in her heart.

He sighed, and regret crept into his eyes. "I haven't thought about how I'm going to say it, so it's probably going to sound—"

"By all means, confess, already."

"What did I do to deserve you?" He threatened a smile. "Why haven't you run back home?"

"Is that what you want?"

"Are you serious, Nicki? No."

She cuddled against him, taking in the loamy green of the water and the palms towering above them. South Florida had a distinct, thriving scent, and breathing was a pleasure. She looked up and met his warm gaze. "I gave you less than twelve hours' notice when I came. If it was

105

a bad time, you'd tell me, right?"

"I've never heard anyone cry the way you did that night." He gave a small shrug with the shoulder she was laying on. "It wasn't a question of the right or wrong time. It was just...time. For a lot of things."

"For us?"

He dropped his hand to her thigh. "Remind me to take you Venice some day."

"Take me to Venice some day." Yes, she wanted to go to Venice with this man...wanted to go to Paris, Madrid, Sydney, and Tokyo. She'd share a ride to the moon, given the chance, but she'd be happier than a kitten in catnip to stay forever in their own little corner on the Isle of Venice.

"That's what brought me here actually. Venice." He nodded toward the front of the taxi. "We're heading out toward the ocean now, but before we reach A1A, we'll clip to the north, and that's when you'll feel it."

"Feel what?"

"Venice. Ever see a picture of it?"

"Sure."

"Well, the intracoastal is something like Venice's canals. We can travel by water over a good portion of the city. There are two-hundred-sixty miles of inland waterways here, and at times it's so tranquil it's hard to believe there's a city surrounding you. The intracoastal is quaint in places, like Old World Europe—Mediterranean and Spanish architecture included."

"But no gondolas."

He shook his head and cracked his half smile. "No, Nicki, but there's nothing we can do on a gondola we can't do on a water taxi after sundown." The hand on her thigh climbed higher.

*   *   *

He'd never made love on gondola, but to be fair, he'd been laid on one. The experience paled in comparison to that of holding Nicki for the whole world to see. For all the soul searching he'd done about his growing feelings for her, being her lover certainly had its advantages.

She loved to please him, in and out of the bedroom, and she appreciated beautiful things. No greater flattery existed than the attention of a woman like her. And he loved it. He loved lots of things about her—her body, her mind, her passion. Her... "Tiny pink panties."

"Pardon me?"

"Tiny pink panties. That's what you're wearing."

She glanced at the water taxi driver, who navigated the boat along the canal in silence, and then addressed Ty with only her eyes.

"It's just a guess." He shrugged, but contrary to what he'd said, he was certain he was dead-on right.

"Sure of yourself, aren't you?"

"Well, yeah. You're methodical, and you're tried-and-true. You're the type of woman who has a favorite shade of lipstick you'll travel ten miles out of your way for. So you probably stick with what works. And for you, that's tiny."

"Dubious. All panties are tiny in comparison with other articles of clothing."

"Not all are thongs. The thong isn't for everyone. And I'm not talking about the discomfort of the string and a woman's decision to wear one or not. I'm saying that not everyone should wear one. Some asses aren't worthy enough. But yours... yours won't quit."

She rolled her eyes. "Point being?"

"Point being that, in addition to being methodical, you're confident. You dress to flatter yourself, and most of your wardrobe has no tolerance for panty lines. Thus, the thong. Tiny."

A small flash of a smile darted across her face, and she nudged him.

"Now, pink. You like things neat and orderly. You're always perfectly put together and coordinated. You wouldn't last any longer in panties that don't match your bra than you would in a dust-covered house, and I see your bra is pink." He tucked a peeking strap under her sundress and placed his hand back on her thigh. "So there you have it. Tiny, pink panties." He mindlessly gathered her dress between his fingers.

"You're proud of yourself." Her hands stopped his from exploring further, but only after he'd nearly reached the panties in question. "Want a medal for that deduction?"

"I can't help myself." He leaned to her lips. "I have an ongoing love affair with lingerie."

"Really. I'd have guessed it to be with your car."

He lingered at her mouth. "Maybe we should put the two together."

"Great idea. You wear the underwear. I'll drive."

A deep kiss distracted him from his protest. Damn, she was a pleasant diversion from his life's recent course. Sweet enough to kiss the car keys—hell, the title—out from under him. It was no wonder he couldn't tell her about Mandy's baby. He stood to lose plenty: a clean house, good food, incredible, earth-shattering sex. Maybe even the chance to love with all he had.

She was the best model he'd ever drawn, and while he enjoyed the simple pleasure of viewing her, pencil in hand or not, he couldn't believe the artistic outpouring she'd inspired in him. Drawing had always been something with which he'd passed idle time, but now it was so much more.

Suddenly, art was an expression of sexuality, fiery desire. Drawing represented passion, and she was the cause of it all. She was flesh, she was life, she was the future.

*   *   *

"I want to see it," Ty said, just before she entered a fitting room.

"Too bad." She zipped the curtain along the rod.

He caught it before it closed and flashed that thrilling smile. "I want to see it."

"I don't parade around in nighties in shopping malls." She yanked on the curtain again, closing it all the way. Although she didn't need it, and couldn't afford it, she hung the garment, floor length and rose-colored silk, on a hook and began to undress.

The silk was cut on a bias so it hugged her every curve. A slit traveled up the left side to high on her thigh, and an understated scoop neck enhanced her generous bust line. Twin spaghetti straps led to a low-cut back, edged with ribbon roses.

It was made for her; it drew attention away from what she considered her too-thick hips, but at its ticket price, it would undoubtedly remain on the rack. She began to take it off.

"Does it fit?" he asked from outside the curtain.

"Perfectly, but—"

"I want to see it."

"Something about it isn't right." She emerged from the fitting room, carrying the lingerie and smoothing her hair.

"Don't put it back," he said.

Clink. The metal hanger hooked onto the rack.

*   *   *

It wasn't really for her anyway. It was *his* birthday, and he wanted it. He thought she could wear it later and pose for him in the unruly garden. Maybe he'd catch her wearing it in the kitchen someday.

In late autumn, maybe early winter, just when the weather dipped below seventy, he would come home from work to find her lounging in a cherry Windsor chair he didn't yet own, feet propped on the kitchen table he didn't have yet either, tapping a pencil against her succulent lips as she studied a blueprint. She'd be baking bread—cinnamon rolls, maybe—and she'd be wearing that nightie.

The terra cotta tile he had yet to install would be cool against her adorable, bare feet when she rose to tend the oven, and he'd catch her halfway there, spin her around in his arms. Let the bread burn. He'd find his way beneath that silk.

He blinked away the daydream. "You really didn't like it?"

"No, I loved it, but...I'd never wear it."

"You'd wear it. Never for long, but you'd wear it."

She laughed and took his hand.

"I want to show you something I've been saving for." He led her to an escalator. "For my kitchen."

"Are you saying we're about to finish the kitchen?" Her eyes brightened with her smile.

"I'm thinking of cherry cabinetry," he said as they exited the escalator at the next level. "With a warm stain. Like this."

They stopped in front of a furniture store, and there in the window display were a bow back Windsor chair and a forty-eight inch round cherry table, Early American style, draped with a white-and-yellow striped cloth.

"Love it." She entered the store.

She didn't stop at the window to peruse the table, but made a beeline for the closest sales associate, who happened to be male, and offered her hand. "Nicolette Paige with Diamond Custom Homes. I have a client interested in the George Wythe Collection you have on display, and if all goes well with this project, we may showcase your pieces in our Oceanview Jewel Box, Key Award winner."

Ty sat on an oversized leather recliner, making himself as invisible as possible, and watched her work. She asked all the right questions, at all the right moments, and she mixed professionalism and sex appeal as precisely as a bartender mixed a martini. She knew design, she knew furniture, and she knew her client well. Observing her in her milieu was nothing short of a pleasure.

And speaking of pleasure, how great would it be to prop her atop that table and slide his fingers along the contours of her breasts? He'd lick her from her tummy to her inner thighs, breathe onto her, into her. Let his hot tongue dance against her delicate skin.

That's what he'd do, all right. Tease her like flames licking a wooden wall. Tickle her into a tirade until she begged for him to finish the job. And he'd finish it, but with more of the same. With small, provoking thrusts that would never completely fill her.

She'd beg him to bring her all the way there, and he'd do it, that's for sure. He'd bring her there, back again, and take her on a revolving trip.

"Ready?" She stashed a color sample into her purse.

Sure, he was ready. Ready to put his most indecent thoughts into action. Right there in the Galleria.

"The table is perfect," she said, "and they gave me a professional discount voucher. But I'm concerned about the cabinetry. Cherry is a finicky wood."

"Cherry is...what?"

"Finicky. It darkens with age. Come on. I'm done."

She didn't expect him to stand up *now*, did she? In his rather...happy...condition, he didn't know if he could.

"Unless there's something else you wanted me to see?"

Well, there was quite a bit *he* wanted to see. Her in that silk nightgown was at the top of the list. But he stood anyway and took her hand. "No. We can go."

On the way out, she stopped to eye the table and turned toward him. "This table's been here for a few months...I asked. So it's fully aged. But the cabinetry might not age the same way. Or at the same rate. We shouldn't try to match the stain because we'll miss."

He nodded. "Come here a second."

"It's your kitchen, so if I'm suggesting something you—"

"Come here." He lifted her and swung her around, depositing her on the tabletop. Her eyes widened and her lips parted in surprise.

Yeah, she looked good up there.

"What are you—"

"Just testing." Dizzy with the thought of what he might someday do on that George Wythe table, he kissed her.

"We're in a window display," she said against his lips.

"So let the world watch."

She hopped to the floor. "Here's what we should do," she said, laughing. "This is Florida, for God's sake, so we can go wild with color. Let's use paint. Pale yellow, or maybe pear green, on the perimeter—glazed, of course—and cherry for the serving pantry and island."

"I have an island?"

"Not yet, but I think you should. You have the space. And as for the appliances, wood panels."

"I was thinking more stainless."

"Of course you were, but forget it. You don't want to clean the fingerprints of eight or nine children off stainless steel."

"Let's discuss it over lunch on Las Olas." He dug in his pocket for his wallet and handed her a five. "Do me a favor. I have an order to check on, so let's meet for coffee in the food court."

Not more than fifteen minutes later, he entered the food court and saw her immediately. She sat with a boy no older than six, who stopped talking only long enough to lick his ice cream cone. Nicki rolled up the child's sleeve and wiped a stream of blue ice cream from his hand.

"Hi."

She looked up. "Ty, this is Mason. Mason, this is my friend, Ty."

Ty nodded and took a seat, placing his shopping bags at his feet. "How long was I gone? You have a kid now?"

She smiled. "His mom's changing a diaper. I said I'd watch him. What'd you buy?"

"It's a surprise."

Mason rambled on about the latest action hero figurine his mother had purchased for him, and Nicki nodded intently, every now and then sopping up melted ice cream.

She'd be a good mother someday. His gaze trailed to her flat tummy, and he couldn't help but wonder what might someday happen.

"Thanks, Nicki." Ty heard an unfamiliar woman's voice and snapped out of his daze to see a rotund woman with a toddler on her hip.

"No problem." Nicki stood and tousled the boy's shaggy brown hair. "It was nice talking to you, Mason."

"Complete strangers trust you with their children," he said, shifting the shopping bag handles between his fingers.

"I must have that look about me that says 'child friendly.'"

So you're a child-friendly environment. Let's go make us some babies.

CHAPTER 12

They disembarked from the water taxi at Las Olas Boulevard on Navarro Isle and, with his arm around her, silently strolled down the sidewalk. "This street reminds me of you. I've been meaning to bring you here for a long time."

"Yeah. I discovered it on my own."

He smiled, allowing his hand to fall lower on her hip. No panty lines to be felt. Tiny and pink, and damned if he wasn't going to prove it to himself later. "There's an art center down the road a piece. I called, and they're sponsoring a student exhibit this week, and...Oh, we're here."

A chalkboard easel boasting the daily specials—Brie en Croute, Calamari Frit, Grilled Swordfish Bourbonnaise—pointed the way down a narrow, red brick walk off the main path, leading to a private, shuttered courtyard. A scattering of tables dotted the brick patio. A man of about sixty occupied a table in an inconspicuous corner, sipping a whiskey on the rocks, engrossed in a worn book of poetry.

"Here we are, Nicki. Las Olas Café."

In the center of the courtyard, aged, deciduous trees stretched toward the heavens, their branches reaching to the far ends of the property, like a mother protecting her young beneath. Strings of white, twinkling lights spiraled about their trunks, emitting a glow in the early afternoon shade.

She grinned. "Hidden treasure indeed."

He pulled out a chair and she sat, crossed her left ankle over her right, and folded her hands in her lap. "I'd draw you like this," he whispered.

She met his gaze. "Pardon?"

"I said if I had my sketch book, I'd draw you." He joined her at the table. "Like this."

She gave her pretty eyes a roll. "I'm sure I'm a million ways undone."

"I only wish." Unable to stop the smile creeping onto his face, he reached for her hand. "There are no words to describe how amazing you look when I've just had my way with you."

Her cheeks flushed, and her lips parted as if she were about to challenge him, but she smiled softly and didn't say a word.

"I love Las Olas Boulevard," he said. "I've seen people tap dancing on the sidewalk, or painting, or photographing something, anything."

"Utopia."

"I'm not surprised you like it. The day I found this place, I saw a young couple drawing with sidewalk chalk right outside. So I thought of you. And two days later, you showed up at my job site."

Suddenly, she seemed to be staring directly into his soul. She took a deep breath and offered her hand, palm up.

"It was as if I called you here." He took her hand. "I had a real sense of place and family back home. When you're a kid, you trust in the things that are constant. My parents, the twins, our house on Claremont. And the little girl from across the street, who'd never leave me alone."

She laughed. "Maybe my sense of place and family was the same as yours. Did you ever think of that?"

"You're not the same little girl anymore, and I'm no longer the guy who used to entertain you with chalk renderings of fairy tales on Claremont sidewalks. I look at you and I see you've grown up—you've definitely filled out—and now, finally, I'm ready to grow, too."

"You already have. You're happier here than I remember you being back home. Talk about filling out—you have. Not only physically, but emotionally. There are more facets to you than anyone's explored. Do you know how intriguing that is?"

"I think you have that effect on me."

"You give me too much credit."

"Do I?"

The old man coughed behind his poetry book and sipped his whiskey. Ty nodded toward him. "He's stolen more glances at the back of your head than a bum has cigarettes. Men love you. Guys of all ages. That kid with the ice cream, the furniture salesman. Christ, that idiot Tabor lugged drywall up my stairs for you, and he's the laziest son-of-a-bitch in south Florida. Men know…they can see just how lucky I am."

She began to shake her head, but returned to her statue-still position in half a second. "We've had a nice day. Maybe you're gilding the lily."

"Let's get a second opinion." He again looked toward the old man and raised his voice. "I'd be crazy not to recognize now as the time, wouldn't I, Ruben?"

The old man raised his glass. "I'll drink to that."

Nicki looked over her shoulder as the old man spoke, and when her gaze returned, a look of astonished amusement was in her eyes.

"Truth is," Ty said, "he'd probably drink to anything, but that doesn't make it any less apparent. So here's what I propose. A bottle of coastal chardonnay with the best seafood on the boulevard. And this." He reached into one of the shopping bags at his feet and pulled out a pink-and-white floral bikini.

"A swim suit?"

"Yeah. I know you have a couple, but Florida girls have tons of them, in every color, shape, and style imaginable. Consider this a jump start on the assortment you'll collect over the years. Assuming, of course, you decide to stay."

*   *   *

She stared at him, fingered the pink Lycra strap of the bikini and closed her gaping mouth. He didn't blink. He didn't smile. Just rubbed at the callus on his thumb, awaiting her reply.

"Are you asking me to…" No more words would form on her tongue, and she fought the urge to lunge across the table and tackle him onto the bricks, kissing him all over.

"I've realized something." His voice lowered to just above a whisper. "I haven't only missed you these past couple of years. I've been lonely without you. Incomplete. I used protect you from men like me. Who knew that eventually I'd be wishing you'd fall for me?"

She had fallen already, but she couldn't find the words to tell him. It seemed such an intangible dream. Was he asking her to stay? To love him?

"You know me. You know my history with women. I can be a jerk when I feel like it, I fight dirtier than grunge, and when it comes to revering you, I can be just plain ignorant. It's a given I'm going to screw up from time to time. You've seen me with women. I don't have staying power, am I right? I mean, there's a reason my file of ex-girlfriends is ten inches thick."

Who was he trying to kid? *Staying power?* If he hadn't stayed with a woman in the past, it was because he'd wanted it that way, not because he didn't have what it took to keep her. She was about to tell him so, but he spoke again.

"I'll forget to tell you how great you smell, how I appreciate your sleepy eyes at the first sign of sunrise. I'll draw you when you're feeling fat, and if you're nagging me to do something I should've finished a month ago, I might ask if it's because you're feeling fat. And you'll probably have to straighten my underwear drawer a few times a week because I don't believe in folding clothes."

The darling café blurred around her, but she was keenly aware of every sound, every scent. The pages of a musty book turned at the remote table behind her. Silverware clanged against dishes inside the dining room door, slicing swordfish, piercing shrimp. A bird shrilled in the leaves above her, and she swore she heard the ocean in the distance.

But she saw nothing but him. Blue eyes deep and sparkling. Full lips in a straight line. Fidgeting, creative hands demonstrating a nervousness he rarely revealed.

"You're going to drive my Betty, throw away my work shirts just because they're torn, and bitch when I track half the dirt of a job site across your clean floor. You'll fill my closet with things you'll never wear, and you'll kick me, punch me, beat me to a pulp in your sleep."

His hands stilled, and a piercing gaze filtered through her like a rush of butterflies.

"I'm fine with all of it, Nicki. I accept it, but I can't accept you leaving me. Ever. You've made such a difference in my life, and I know you deserve so much more, but I can't let you go."

She'd heard every syllable, and there were countless words she wanted to say in return. But she couldn't stop her head from spinning, couldn't catch her breath. She was articulate, damn it. Why couldn't she form a sentence?

All of her parts tingled as if she were about to have an orgasm. Quite possibly, she would. Right there, in the Las Olas Café courtyard, when no one had laid a hand on her. But who could blame her? He'd touched her in another way—with his heart. And physical gratification couldn't compare to the fulfillment she now felt. With a slight tremor, she rose from her chair.

"Nicki, I—"

She leaned across the table and, cupping his face in her hands, kissed him with every ounce of love within her.

With a hand on her elbow, he guided her around the table and into his lap. He held her fast, his strong hands at her back, steadying her against the dizzying, whirling world around her.

Heat sizzled through the cleft between her legs, her breasts tingled with anticipation, but even the physical pleasure was no match for the emotions stirring within her. The union of their tongues represented a permanence she'd never known possible. This was it. Forever.

When she broke the kiss and opened her eyes, he dragged a large finger from her cheek to her chin. The right corner of his mouth crept into a smile, and simultaneously, they exhaled.

She was home.

*   *   *

Perched on a dock along the intracoastal canal, with a longneck bottle for company, Ty sketched Nicki from a distance.

She'd poured herself a glass of wine and camped in the garden. His appliance list and the kitchen plans she'd sketched were carefully laid on the table in front of her, held in place with stones she'd found in the overgrown foliage.

It was late afternoon, tranquil—a perfect moment to study his girl from a distance and to record her beautiful figure on paper. This time, he used artistic license, drawing her in her present position at the table, but in lieu of the dress, he drew the elegant negligee she'd refused at the Galleria.

In his sketch book, satin billowed among groomed plants, her nipples were taut, and there was nothing but a glass of wine on the table before her. A stray tendril drooped in a spiral at her temple, and the ring on her fourth toe caught a ray of sunset, sparkling.

The gurgling sound of an approaching boat threatened to pull him from the daydream, but he closed his eyes and concentrated.

In his mind, this picture was the prelude to a romantic event. Maybe he wouldn't have the patience to take her inside. Maybe he'd make love to her right there.

"Hey, Carmichael."

He blinked away from his reverie and the scenario faded.

"Quite an imagination you have there."

Ty turned to greet the man who deserved no acknowledgement at all. Tabor stood—all five feet, six inches of him—in his speedboat, bobbing alongside the dock, staring over Ty's shoulder at his sketch book.

"Hendricks Isle is on the other side of the canal," Ty said, turning back toward the garden.

"She's something, isn't she?" Tabor whistled behind him.

"A convenience store has maps. West of the canal is your plot of land, but east is the Isle of Venice. You're on my property."

"Waterways are public."

"Yeah, well, you're getting too close for comfort."

"Your place still torn apart?"

"It's a work in progress." Ty didn't want to look at him, but he glanced anyway and cringed. He'd love to smack a fist into Tabor's jaw, but he wasn't worth the trouble. "And she sees beyond the dust."

"I don't know about that. She seemed pretty eager to clean it up the day I met her."

"Hendricks Isle. Right behind you."

"Have to hand it to you, Carmichael. Sweet little piece you got there. She's never wearing much, and I catch a few glimpses from time to time."

His stomach knotted with the thought of Tabor's eyes violating the perfection of Nicki's body. *He's all talk anyway. He didn't see a thing.* "Here's an official warning not to look again."

"You got to work sometime, don't you? What she does on her own time is her own business. Just ask your last girlfriend."

Ty shook his head, refusing to take the bait. Why did women find this jerk attractive? He lived on his daddy's money and didn't even have a job. He turned back to his sketchpad.

Tabor sniffed. "When you gonna own up to that baby anyway?"

"I should be asking you the same question."

"I'm too good to make a mistake like that, my friend."

Ty's shoulders tensed, but he was done entertaining Tabor.

"Guess I'll be going."

"Why don't you do that?" Ty didn't turn around when the boat sputtered into motion. As long as he kept his eyes on Nicki, the tranquility of the day remained.

She pressed her cell phone to her ear and poised a pen against the house plans. Her mother was on the other end of that call. Or perhaps it was her roommate. She was doing what he knew he had to do, too—tying up the loose ends of the life she'd lived before this life with him on the Isle of Venice.

Contrary to his firm belief, she had not brought everything she owned to south Florida. Hopefully she'd convince her mother to send the essentials—apparently, three suitcases were not enough to hold the important things she owned.

But that was only the beginning. Her apartment, her house plants—everything needed to be resolved in Chicago. And then there was the matter of a job here. She'd certainly proven her worth in taking part in a Key-winning project, but Ray Diamond had yet to extend an offer.

She could always find work at local studios, but now more than ever, he didn't want her to pose. He understood, at last, why it was important to her, but that didn't change his dislike of it. There would always be students more interested in her sexuality than in art. There would always be those assuming she was less of a lady because she took her clothes off for money. For a moment, he considered calling his father and begging him to write the letter of commendation Nicki had earned. With Robert Carmichael's backing, she was sure to land a job at a design showroom of her choosing.

And the paternity suit was another obstacle. If he was wrong about Mandy's baby, which he wasn't, he and Nicki wouldn't only have couplehood to adjust to—he'd have a new identity. He'd be someone's father, and Nicki would have to be okay with it. That was a lot to ask of anyone. Hell, it was a lot to ask of himself.

*　　　*　　　*

"Nicki, staying there will be the biggest mistake of your life," Jeanine lectured over the telephone. "Get your body on the next flight out of there."

"I belong here," Nicki said, gazing out over the intracoastal waterway. The setting sun fell upon the canal in tawny ripples. Ty waved from the docks, and she returned the salutation. "I've never felt this right about anything."

"Of course you haven't. You're probably sleeping with him, aren't you?"

Nicki didn't answer. Her sex life was no business of her mother's, but silence only conveyed the truth.

"For heaven sakes." Her mother gave a dramatic sigh. "Not six months ago, I dragged your brothers and Carl through that dirty city of yours—"

"It was your city, too, once upon a time."

"—to an engagement party in your honor. Do you know how difficult it is to drag a two-year-old and a baby through six inches of snow down Michigan Avenue, keep them quiet and contained in a tiny, over-priced apartment belonging to some stuffed shirt, only to wish a stranger well in marrying your daughter?"

Nicki rested her forehead in her hand. "No."

"Well, I did it, and I did it for you. Pardon my lack of enthusiasm when you tell me you're dropping one dumb-stick for another."

"It didn't happen that way."

"And Ty Carmichael, Nicki? Have you forgotten his reputation? Do you want to end up unmarried, pregnant, and alone in a place you don't belong? Believe me, it's not a good life to live. For you or your child. You should know that by now."

"Stop drawing parallels. You were seventeen when you had me, and you didn't know my father very well, but I know Ty better than anyone."

"Someone needs to remind you—"

"And as far as his reputation goes, he's always taken care of me. Doesn't that mean anything to you? Comfort you in any way?"

"Your attachment to that man has always been unnatural."

"Why? Because you didn't understand it? He gave me what you weren't interested in giving me—stability and someone to talk to."

"Then maybe it's his interest in you that's unnatural. What does his family think of this?"

Nicki sipped her wine and sighed again. "Are you going to send my things or not?"

Her half-brothers' wailing in the background filled a moment that might have been spent in silent thought. "I can't condone what you're doing, Nicki. If you want your things, you'll have to make other arrangements."

"Thanks." A balmy, whispering breeze swept through her hair, and she breathed in the scent of south Florida—jasmine and ocean, vines and loam. "Can I say one more thing?"

"I don't know if I have the stomach for it right now. Carl's late, your brothers are out of their minds..."

"You have a life that doesn't involve me, and I've done more than understand why. I'm glad you're happy, glad you found a chance to start over and have what you've always wanted. Can't you extend the same courtesy to me?"

"Nicki, I have my hands full. I'll speak to you when you get home."

Click. She looked at her cell phone for a moment before snapping it closed. So much for parental support.

A kiss sizzled on her shoulder and the tension in her back eased away. *Don't think about it right now. Enjoy this moment.* She sighed in contentment.

*   *   *

"Mmm."

Damn, he loved that sound. With gentle pressure, he raised her chin and kissed her on the mouth, hoping he'd always be able to kiss away her frowns. "Want to tell me what happened?"

She shook her head. "It's fine. Everything's fine."

"It's going to be." He led her into the house, through the dining room door, and backed her against the wall. "I promise."

With one arm, he lifted her. She wrapped her legs around his waist, and his fingertip explored the terrain beneath her dress.

"What do you know? Tiny panties." He inched them aside, pressed his erection against her. "And will you look at that? Pink."

CHAPTER 13

That night the ocean's dark mysticism was something akin to a fairy princess castle in a seven-year-old's mind—alluring and sparkly. The wet sand squished between Nicki's bare toes, and the warm breeze caressed its way beneath her dress, awakening her every nerve.

Or perhaps the man at her side, carrying her shoes, was responsible for that. Ty sauntered next to her, whistling the same ballad he always sang in the shower, and the surf threatened to tickle her feet, rising to within inches of their path.

The ocean wasn't alone in its contentment. A sense of belonging—something she'd never before felt—swam through her veins. South Florida was her paradise, and Ty Carmichael was her Adam. She loved the way he held her, the way he spoke, the way he made love. They were going to make it. She knew it in her heart.

He stopped and turned toward her. Brushed a tendril from her forehead. Stopped whistling. "Look." He pressed a brief kiss onto her lips.

Out of the corner of her eye, she spotted a trail of Ty's and her footprints reaching far into the horizon.

"Keep looking," he whispered.

She glanced at their footprints head-on. They'd come a long way together, but she didn't need impressions in wet sand to tell her that.

"Now listen," he said.

She heard nothing, and he didn't speak. When she looked at him and began to inquire what she might be listening for, he shook his head and pressed a finger to her lips.

"Shh." He pulled her closer.

She listened, staring up at him, feeling as if she were about to receive the promise of a lifetime.

He wrapped his arms around her, and the surf lapped against the sand like a metronome. Swoosh, splash. Swoosh, splash.

His heart beat in time. Swoosh, splash, bum-bum. Swoosh, splash, bum-bum.

After a few moments, she recognized her breathing as part of the rhythm, too. Swoosh, splash, breath, bum-bum. He brushed his thumb across the small of her back, and she journeyed further into his eyes. Swoosh, splash, breath, bum-bum, brush. A magical night in a mystifying locale. Her home. Swoosh, splash, breath, bum-bum, brush.

And just when she thought the cadence had hypnotized her, the ocean rumbled with a whispering roar, and the surf rose, beating the shore with discernibly more strength than before. The wave erased their footprints, chasing the sand to a faraway shore.

"Did you hear that?" He smiled. "That's the ocean's idea of absolute bliss. All the world's pleasures building up from somewhere we can't even see and breaking on the shore. It's something, isn't it? The same rhythm, repetition, concentration. And then, in a heartbeat, it rises. It breaks. Just like a woman on the brink of climax."

And he knew just what a woman coming was like, didn't he? She gazed down the beach.

"We have to talk," he said. "And it won't be easy for either of us."

She found his eyes in the moonlit darkness, felt the heat of his scrutiny. Her head spun with the depth of emotion she found in his gaze. Her heart fluttered, but with anticipation or dread, she couldn't decide.

Had he learned of her posing?

"We need to talk." He glanced away. "But not here."

"Why not?" She rested a hand on his cheek, but he didn't turn toward her for more than a moment.

"Too public."

"We're alone."

"Or so it seems." He took her hand and led her back the way they had come and nodded in the direction of Route A1A. "Hard to remember this sanctity exists a few hundred feet from the nightlife of a city, but it does."

*   *   *

Once he'd decided it was time to tell her about Mandy's baby, he rushed toward the Isle of Venice, eager to have it done. She matched his stride, two to one, a look of concern in her eyes.

His forthcoming news would burden her with uncertainty. Hot off the press, it might wound her vivacious soul. She trusted him, and he'd been far from honest. He hadn't lied, per se, but he'd kept an important piece of the puzzle from her, allowed her to make the decision to stay with him before telling her a baby may be popping in every other weekend for visitation. For the rest of their lives.

A baby. God, a baby was forever. There was a good chance—well, a snippet of a chance, anyway—that Mandy's baby might be part of his life long after Nicki left it, if this news was too much for her to handle.

With the thought of it, a heaviness settled in his chest, and he stopped abruptly to face her. She stumbled into him, and although he attempted to catch her, she fell to the sand.

The sight of her lounging figure, one bent knee draped against the other, wet sand clinging to her gingham dress as if she were a tease of a centerfold, chased away the weight of his conscience. He felt a smile coming on, and when she reached up, he extended his hand and helped her to her feet. "Falling for me?"

"More like tripping over you."

He rubbed sand from her shoulders, and off her back and bottom. Hmm, good place to keep his hands. On her perfect rear end. "What makes you so tough?"

"Tough?" She shook her head. "Not in the least."

"You know what a gem you are, even when everyone's treating you like gravel." He gathered the dress between his fingers and sighed against her lips, walking her dress into his hands, ready to pull it off. "You know what you like, what you want. You know what you deserve."

"And that might be?"

"The same thing I've been telling you since you were seven years old, standing at that mailbox. You deserve nothing short of everything."

She stared up at him, fingering a loose curl before tucking it behind her ear. It was nothing he hadn't said a thousand times before, but for the first time, she listened as if realizing he meant every word.

Her breasts brushed against his chest amid a deep breath. "Whatever we have to talk about, whatever you have to say, we'll be all right." She kissed him, sweeping her tongue against his in a manner both flirtatious and elegant. "Won't we?"

With the moonlight on her curves, she looked heavenly. His body reacted the way it always did when studying her—hardening everywhere from his chest and forearms to those parts more obviously affected.

When they reached Las Olas Boulevard, he dropped her shoes on the broadwalk, scattering sand from their soles.

"Thanks," she said, perching on the wave wall and brushing sand from her dress.

He crouched before her and took her feet into his hands, rubbing her arches from heels to toes, sprinkling white grains onto the bricks beneath them. How easy it would be to let his hands wander beneath her dress. If he stayed close enough, no one would be the wiser. And considering what he was about to tell her, it might be his last chance to touch her in an intimate manner.

She stared at him as if she wanted him to touch her. He was no stranger to the look in her eyes, and seeing it made him even more determined to bury a finger in the silky pocket between her legs.

If he casually slid a hand up her inner thigh, his little finger would be in there in half a second. He could almost feel the grip of her tunnel, dripping sweetness around his digit. And who would know?

She breathed deeply, her breasts rising with a subtle surge of passion, and her lower lip hung in the delectable pout that told him it was time. Time to kiss her, time to make love to her, time to fulfill her every fantasy. His hand began to climb.

"Nicki, hi."

He whipped his head toward the voice and met the gaze of an eccentric woman with Buddy Holly glasses and bright orange hair, with a plain-faced, barrel-shaped woman on her arm.

"Annie." Nicki stood, her hand resting on his shoulder. "This is Ty."

He nodded, trying with all his might not to stare.

"This is my model," Annie said to her companion. "Nicki Paige."

And suddenly, the odd couple didn't rate. He looked up at Nicki, fire and disappointment clogging his throat. *Model?*

"Nicki, this is my partner, Myke."

When Nicki's hand left Ty's shoulder, he gathered the strength to stand and force a smile.

"The student exhibit's up and running. Seen it yet?" Annie asked.

"I stopped by." Nicki reached for Ty's hand, and while he allowed her to take it, he did not wrap his fingers around hers.

Annie placed a hand over her heart. "My, did they capture you."

"We'll put it on our agenda," Ty said. "It's always a pleasure to see how strangers interpret my good fortune."

"Good seeing you," Nicki said. "And nice meeting you, Myke."

Ty shook free from her hand and started down Las Olas. "You're modeling."

"I'm sorry I didn't tell you." Her heels clicked alongside him. "But I figured since she's a woman—"

"A lesbian."

"Whatever. I didn't know Myke was a she until two minutes ago, and Annie's gig came with strings attached. Two studio sessions per week."

"The one thing I asked you not to do."

"But it's what I do."

"You design."

"I'm not good at design. Your father made that perfectly clear. But I'm a good model. You said so yourself."

"Nicki, don't put an ounce of faith into what my father said. He—"

"He's a repeat Custom Homebuilder of the Year. He knows a good designer when he sees one."

"You're a good designer. You have no business taking your clothes off when you can easily work in a showroom."

"Have I asked you to stay off your job site? No, and you had no right to ask me to stay off mine."

"There's an entire exhibit of my nude girlfriend at the Las Olas Art Center, and I'm supposed to be okay with it?"

"Not an entire exhibit. Just one piece."

"And that makes it all right?" He spun to face her. "Nicki, you're making a fool of me."

"No, you're making a fool of yourself. Have some faith in me, will you? The way I believe in you. I held your hand until you won that Key, and you—"

"This isn't about me or my endeavor to—"

"That's where you're wrong, Ty. It's always about you. You make my posing your business. You make it your decision. You don't care that I feel competent, beautiful, revered on a pedestal. You only care that it makes you feel like less of a man."

"That's not true."

Her right eyebrow shot up. "Isn't it?"

"I've explained this time and again. It's about the way others

125

perceive you."

"And you think I care about the opinions of the ignorant?"

"Do you care about my opinion?"

"You want me to stop, but it's part of me."

"A part you don't need."

"Unless you're the artist drawing me?"

He fixated on her decadent mouth. Was it wrong to keep her for himself, to protect her from a cruel world?

"I..." With a knit brow, she gave her head a minute shake. "I can't do this."

"What?"

"I'll never measure up to your expectations if you can't accept this."

"My expectations? Nicki—"

"I can't."

"You awaken me, Nicki." He met her gaze. "The images you lure out of me...how do I know you won't arouse another man that way?"

"Maybe I'll inspire someone else, but that doesn't mean he'll inspire me."

"There's no 'maybe' about what you stir in a man, any man. I mean, look at you. You're beautiful."

"I don't feel beautiful when you assume I'll open my legs for anyone who sketches my body." Wisdom flickered in her somber eyes, along with a glistening tear.

He turned away for a moment, unwilling to watch her cry, but she'd ensnared him. He didn't have a choice; he had to look at her.

"That's what you're doing, you know." She wiped the lone tear from her cheek. "You're assuming I feel for all of them what I feel for you."

"No. But you should've told me." He brushed a tendril from her forehead, thoughts of what *he'd* yet to tell *her* a fraying rope in his mind.

"You should've made the news more welcome."

"Maybe," he whispered, closing the gap between them. "But you can't make me like what you do."

"Who says you have to? Support my decision to do it, whether you hate it or not. I support everything you do. Everything. And not because I'm sleeping with you, but because I want you to smile every day."

Why did she have an answer for everything? And why did she have to make sense? He brushed a thumb against her chin. "I want you to smile every day, too."

She leaned to him and laid her mouth on his. A perfect fit.

"I mean that," he said against her lips. He trailed one hand to her back, holding her tight, and the slightest, most delightful tremor shimmied through her. The scent of fresh ocean air drifted from her hair, and the noise of A1A buzzed in his ears, reminders of where they stood. *Well, let all of south Florida watch.* He loved her, and he didn't care who knew it.

Loved her? Suddenly, it seemed he had two things to confess.

He broke the kiss, at last looking into her eyes. Yes, he loved her. Loved her from the golden curls spilling about her face to the faux pink topaz in her toe ring. Loved her *café au lait* eyes, her long, slender legs, and, God, he loved her breasts.

He loved the creative side of her mind, her obsessive attitude about cleanliness, the way children were drawn to her. And as he stared down at her, he realized he'd probably loved her for years.

*   *   *

He pulled the dress from her body and tossed it aside.

The plush comforter cradled her body, clad only in scraps of silk and spandex, and a soft breeze feathered in the window. She reveled in the bed's luxury, watching him inch the shirt off his chest above her.

He climbed onto the bed and leaned over her, a callused hand traveling south along her side and coming to rest on her hip with the hint of a squeeze.

Ever-present between her legs, his erection threatened to burst through his boxers, but he made no movement to rush things, save a slow, steady gyration of his hips that dared to drive her insane. She wrapped her legs around his waist, but to no avail.

His skilled lips traveled to her neck, where he placed long, precise kisses against her. He nestled between her breasts and whispered against her lingerie. She couldn't understand what he was saying, whether he was saying anything at all, but it felt like heaven.

He kissed her full on the mouth and cupped her rear in his hand. From behind, a finger tickled her against her panties, and he sighed from deep within his throat.

She laced one hand into his unruly hair and the other sought his boxers. But he caught her before she reached him and pinned her wrist into the pillows, kissing her all the while.

And fanning the flames higher, a few fingers wiggled beneath her panties, taunting her with the promise of pleasure, but not allowing her to indulge.

"You're teasing me." She sounded desperate and breathless, not at all like herself.

His smile flashed at her. "Yeah."

"Stop."

"No." He lowered his lips to hers, still tantalizing her nether regions with the tip of one finger after another, some entering, others lingering.

"Ty."

"Nicki?" He kissed her. "Shut up." The pressure of his fingers relented. He was playing a game she didn't know how to win.

"Ty," she whispered, on the verge of pleading. He was hardly doing himself any favors by delaying the inevitable. Judging by the way he pressed against her, he needed her as much as she needed him.

After a quick nip on her neck, he zapped her with a concentrated stare. "I promise, Nicki. I'm gonna get you there."

She was just about to smile when a breeze passed between their bodies, leaving her trembling in a dewy shiver.

He moved away. *Liar!*

But he tongued a path from her shoulder to her wrist and back again, that damn little finger still pulsing against her opening in a mischievous dance that heightened her senses, made her even more aware of his mouth, now roving over her stomach. Her skin might have burst into flames, if not for the breeze caressing them.

A tiny, devilish smile appeared in his lips before he slipped his mouth to her inner thigh, breathing against the most private part of her, but keeping a safe distance from biting into her.

When he finally flattened his tongue against her panties, it was with a rhythm designed to take her breath away. He brushed her up and down, rippling into her with subtle force enough to blind her. He wove his tongue beneath her thong.

*   *   *

Hers was the nectar and texture of a peach. His tongue delved deeper, drinking from her, tasting every inch.

She tensed her fingers in his hair and her thighs around his head. Her pulse raced against his tongue; he pressed a finger inside her, rubbing, dragging pleasure out of her, nudging her higher.

He memorized the glory of her body, the taste of her, as if this were to be his last pleasure. And it very well could be, considering the news he had to share.

Her breath began to catch, and a dollop of sugar burst within her. He pressed a hand to her tummy, holding her stationary, lapping against her walls until she relaxed, shaking in an understated quiver.

"Oh, my."

He backed away slowly.

She wiped her left hand across her brow. "My, my, my." Her fingers laced into the curls at the crown of her head, her palm covered one closed eye, and a breathless giggle escaped her. "Oh, my."

She seemed the ultimate in femininity at that moment. Spent, but ready.

"Wait," he said, bounding from the bed. "I want that position."

"Now? Are you—"

"Hold it, hold it, hold it." He scrambled into the closet and dragged a sketchpad off the shelf. "I'll be quick, I promise."

If her eyes had been open, he was sure he'd have seen them roll, but she obliged him with only a small request in return. "I want to see it this time."

"Relax." He honed in on the frame of her face, half-hidden with her hand, striving to capture her nonchalance, the carefree spirit riding through her at the moment. "I'm not going for Mona Lisa on this one, but something about the way you're smiling…"

The charcoal took control, making his thoughts, his feelings take form. He read the satisfaction on her face. Something about her smile, something about her hand, or maybe a combination of the two, set his heart on a drum roll.

Like a flash of neon light, he realized what had caught his attention and swiftly, he scribbled the missing element onto the paper and tossed the sketchpad onto the bed. "There you have it."

She rolled to her side and studied his sketch for a fraction of a second before her brow began to knit in confusion. But soon, she exploded in elation. He smiled along with her.

Her breathless giggle sounded again. "Oh, my."

*   *   *

His smile cracked.

She tumbled into his embrace, sketch in hand. His etchings were far from refined, but the nose was her nose, the smile was her smile, and the hand was her hand. A very realistic representation.

The ring on the fourth finger, however, was none she'd ever worn.

It was a square stone set high and flanked with smaller gems. She knew it was a diamond, set in white gold, bordered by two sapphires. She saw the ring as clearly in her mind as when she'd stumbled across it in his T-shirt drawer. It had been his Great Aunt Evie's. She looked up into his burning blue eyes.

"Is this…" She tried not to break eye contact, but her gaze wandered back to the sketch. "Does this mean…"

"What do you think it means?"

"I think I need an interpretation."

"Go ahead and interpret."

"An interpretation from you."

"Your job as my model is to evoke feelings." He grinned, tickling her ribs. "It's my job as an artist to capture them. And as my audience, Nicki, you interpret it in any way you choose." He rolled her over and stared into her eyes. A crazy spike of bleached blonde hair dropped between his eyes.

"You should explain." She hadn't meant to whisper, but suddenly, speaking succinctly was difficult.

He began to shake his head.

"You should," she said. "I might get the wrong—"

"I think you know exactly what it means."

"I might, but…tell me."

"When I think of forever, I think of you. Suddenly, crazy ideas are popping into my head. Crazy realizations that tell me I love you, that maybe I loved you long before I found a life in south Florida, that maybe I left Chicago because I was afraid you wouldn't love me the way—"

She couldn't listen to another word. Her mouth met his, searching for the forever he mentioned.

"Say something," he said between kisses. "Tell me you love me, too. Tell me I'm crazy—I know I am—but say something."

With a sob escaping her, she cupped his gorgeous face. "You're crazy," she said, kissing him again. "But so am I."

"Remember this," he whispered, his lips lingering at hers. "Whenever you're thinking I'm half the man I should be, remember this moment. Promise me."

How could she forget? He was looking at her as if he never again wanted to let her out of his sight, and he effortlessly worked the clasp on her brassiere, stripping it from her body.

"Promise?" he asked, removing her drenched panties.

"Yes."

He melted kisses from her neck to the mark at her hip. "Something's missing."

"Everything's missing." She shivered.

"I meant"—kiss, kiss, kiss—"something specific." He reached under the bed.

She heard the crinkle of a shopping bag. Had he stashed his purchases under the bed? She'd have to unpack them first thing in the morning.

"So tell me. What about this wasn't right?" The pink negligee shimmered into view, slinking between his fingers. "I'll bet it was perfect, wasn't it?"

"I loved it."

"Let me love you in it."

She ignored her instinct to hand wash the garment first and allowed him to slide it over her head. The material hung against her in all the right places, a comfortable silk blanket against her skin.

"Nice." He studied her. "But still, something's missing."

"Nothing is missing, Ty, except you. Come here."

"No, something's..." He left the bed and crossed his arms over his chest as he squinted down at her. "I know what it is." He meandered toward the highboy and opened a drawer.

Of course. A condom.

When he turned around, however, the item he'd retrieved wasn't one wrapped in red foil. A small velvet box rested in his grasp.

"Oh, my." Her heart raced.

He climbed onto the mattress and opened the box. "Feel like wearing this for a few decades?"

She nodded, but couldn't find voice enough to speak. The diamond entranced her, and she couldn't help staring it. When she heard Ty's chuckle, she managed to take her eyes from the heirloom ring and return his smile.

He slipped the band onto her finger. It fit, as if it were sized for her hand. She wiped a joyful tear from her cheek, and their lips met.

"In case I forget to tell you." He lowered her onto her back, kissing her all the while. "This has been the best birthday ever."

She wrapped her legs around him as he penetrated her with his naked cock. He grazed the diamond with his thumb and stared into her eyes.

CHAPTER 14

Ty's wakefulness had little to do with Nicki's elbows jabbing his sides and her fists punching his arms. This morning, one Key Award Winner would be declared National Custom Homebuilder of the Year. If he'd won, there would be a message from *Custom Home* Magazine on Ray's voice-mail to coordinate interviews and photography. If he'd lost, he wouldn't know to whom until the magazine hit newsstands in the next few weeks.

He knew what it felt like to win. Four golden keys hung in the Carmichael Architectural Design showroom in Chicago. But those awards belonged to his father, and as impeccable as the Oceanview Jewel Box had turned out to be—Nicki had nailed the interior design to perfection—Ty knew the national competition was stiff. Diamond Construction had won Florida's Key Award, but Custom Homebuilder of the Year was a long shot—especially with his father in the running.

Furthermore, his lawyer had called. Two weeks ago, Mandy had given birth to Mia Celeste Washington, but she now refused to gather the baby's DNA sample in order to compare it with Ty's. Obviously, she was stalling, delaying the truth.

But every once in a while, he'd play *What if.* What if Mia's DNA matched his? He'd be a father, not that he knew the first thing about parenting. The thought of being responsible for a tiny person warmed his heart. Could it be he actually wanted the baby to be his?

The beautiful woman next to him sighed in her sleep. "Hmmm." The Chocolate Sea would debut in a few days, and while he'd done his best to be supportive, he often struggled with the prospect of complete strangers knowing Nicki's body in such an intimate fashion.

Whenever he looked at her, he wanted to draw her, and when he drew her, he wanted to make love to her. And worse yet, he knew others—men and women, alike—felt the same way. He crawled from bed and grabbed his sketch pad, ready to capture her, complete with tangled hair and nightgown twisting about her torso.

*   *   *

"So I understand I should extend my congratulations." Verna sat cross-legged in the middle of her sunroom, her fingers working a trail of orange yarn around a crochet hook. "You're having a helluva month, aren't you? The Key Award, the ring you're wearing, and now that kinky sea of body parts got a great write-up in the paper. You should be proud. Those are your parts."

"I hope Ty's really as all right with it as he says." From her post atop a stepladder's second rung, Nicki wiped sweat and old paste from her brow and yanked a tiny shred of wallpaper from the wall.

"I tell you this. If he wants you, but can't have anyone looking at you, it ain't an even balance of power. I love him, baby carrots, but you stick to your guns."

"I can hardly back down now. Geez, what is this wallpaper stuck with? Crazy glue?"

Verna shrugged. "I told Ty not to worry, I'd paint over it."

"Might as well ask the sun not to shine. He's thorough when it comes to home renovation. It's in his blood."

Verna grinned, popping bubble gum between her molars. "Is thorough lovemaking in his blood, too?"

Nicki fought a smile. "What do you think?"

"Honey, I heard women scream his name halfway across this isle. Ain't much left to the imagination on the subject." She blew a tendril of hair from her forehead. "But, tulip patch, I'd be ice skating in hell if I ever said I'd seen him look at a one of them the way he looks at you."

She shook her head. "You don't have to say that. I know he's amazing, I know women love him. I know he's—"

"Oh, I ain't the type of gal to blow a horn just to hear it honk. The very first day I heard him say your name, I knew you was different from all the rest. Something in his eyes sparkles when he thinks about you. It don't do that with the others."

"What about the girl he almost married?"

"Mandy?" Verna waved a hand. "That girl didn't last any longer than a quickie on an altar before Sunday service, though you'd never guess it, what with all that's going on now."

Nicki shook her head, unable to fight her smile. "Have you ever had sex on an altar, Verna?"

The older woman shrugged. "Sure. You?"

"No."

"Ain't missing much. The floor's downright hard, which is all right, I suppose. At my age, something should be." Verna winked, twirling the yarn around her fingers. Her gaze trailed toward the window, along with her crooked index finger. "Look, look, look."

Nicki followed Verna's gaze. "What?"

"Did you see him? Did you?"

"Who?"

"Shoot, he was gone when you looked, wasn't he?" She clenched a fist around a wad of orange yarn and looked to the ground, trembling. "Damn it, George, you're just loving this, letting everyone think I'm crazy. Someone's going to see you sooner or later, so you may as well quit your vanishing."

"Are you all right?" Nicki climbed down from the ladder and stepped around a pile of old fashion magazines.

"He don't know nothing about manners neither." Verna glanced at her, but quickly returned her attention to the ground. "If you was alive and well, you'd be trying to take her pants off. You can't say hello?"

Nicki placed a hand on the older woman's shoulder. "Verna?"

"I'm fine, sweet thing. I'm fine. Just he knows how to get my goat, that's all." She patted Nicki's hand. "Take a break. Have a seat."

Nicki searched the immediate area for something to sit on, but dusty boxes and dirty clothes occupied every piece of worn rattan furniture in the room. She opted for the floor, next to her hostess. "Verna? Can I ask you something? About George?"

Verna shrugged and began to crochet again. "I suppose so."

"I know he hurt you with these other women. Do you think he's coming back to make amends?"

"Ty don't think he's coming back at all. Neither do those ole biddies I hang around. They think it's all up here." She tapped her temple with her index finger.

"Well, I'm not sure, but if you see him, maybe it's because you need to get over the hurt."

"Wasn't nothing left but hurt when he went, Nicki. I got over it ages ago."

"Lovers hurt each other in ways friends can't, but something good comes from it, or no one would ever go through the trouble."

"Honey buns, he gave me five of the most beautiful girls in the world before he started sticking it to random women. And you know what? He lost every single one. Lost the women, lost his girls. He served his own penance, and he don't need to make amends with me. He just likes to crawl under my skin, that's all.

"And let me tell you something. Just between us...I don't so much mind seeing him every now and again. Reminds me I used to be trusting, and now I'm a much better judge of character. That's what I learned from the infidelity of George Davis. I don't know if it's good, but I sure-as-shooting walked away a little smarter now, didn't I?"

Nicki pressed a hand the small of her back, remembering the bruise that had sent her fleeing to Ty's side. "I think I know exactly what you mean."

*   *   *

"Any problems, Carmichael?" Ray Diamond, CEO of Diamond Custom Homes, asked from street level, shading his eyes from the bright sunlight with a rolled-up set of plans.

One story up, Ty pulled a sweat-streaked T-shirt from his body and tucked it through his belt loop. He shook his head. "No problem, Ray. I'm two guys short today, but Montalvo and I worked overtime on Saturday, so we're still on schedule."

"Good. Can't afford not to be with hurricane season upon us. Plenty of nature's delays ahead."

"God, it's hotter than blazes today, isn't it?"

"Welcome to south Florida."

"Will you stop saying that? I live here."

"Hell, even the lizards have been here longer than you. Come on down."

Ty walked to the far side of the roughly framed residence and rushed down the construction stairs, skipping every other one and then bounding off the third to the last to the ground. Nervous energy balled in his gut. Ray was there either for a very good reason, or a very disappointing one. "What's up?"

"You owe me a damn secretary."

Ty was about to plead his case when he realized the general contractor was smiling. He smiled in return. "Yeah, yeah. What else is new?"

"New? I don't know if it's new, but I got a call about seven last night from a big shot editor with *Custom Home* magazine. "

What? Ty twitched a smile. "We got it? We won?"

"You're damn right, Carmichael."

"Great! Great news." He held out his hand and his boss shook it.

"They'll call your cell to schedule an interview, and I hope to hell we're done with the last of the trim work, because we're photographing in two days."

Ty couldn't hide his smile. "Yeah, we're done."

"Bertolli's gonna be drowning his sorrows in an ocean of beer," Ray said.

"Bertolli's too busy with his yacht to pay attention to his company. We can build him out of the box and you know it."

"Until now, we haven't had the projects to prove it."

"Congratulations, Ray."

"What the hell are you congratulating me for? I wouldn't have taken that project if you weren't heading that crew."

"Thanks."

"And I don't know who leaked it, but the word's out." Ray reached into his breast pocket for a cigarette. "I checked messages this morning. Would you believe we've got a dozen new inquiries?" He puffed on the smoke. "We're going to be busier than busy. And damn it, you owe me a secretary."

"She quit of her own volition. That baby's not mine." Not as far as he knew anyway, but even the lingering thoughts of Mandy and her baby weren't enough to dampen his spirits. A Key Award. Custom Homebuilder of the Year. His name would be in print; he'd get partial credit for the honor. And his father was going to see it all.

*   *   *

"Hello." A woman's voice, as musical as the wind chimes sounding in the distance, floated to Nicki's ears from across the sidewalk.

Nicki, rubbing a dried patch of wallpaper paste from her elbow, looked up to see a beautiful woman with the creamiest, peachiest skin she'd ever seen sitting on Ty's porch steps. Her auburn hair was long and flowing, and she wore a sleeveless, tailored pants suit the color of lemon sorbet.

There was nothing quite like running into a perfectly made up superwoman, especially at an inopportune moment such as this. Nicki ran a dirty hand through her even dirtier hair, flecked with old plaster, and sighed. She probably stank of moldy wallpaper and last night's sex, not to mention the stream of sweat dripping between her breasts.

She glanced to the left and then to the right. No one in sight. This brunette Barbie doll was obviously speaking to her, not that she'd doubted it, judging by her position on Ty's porch. "Can I help you?"

"I'm looking for Ty."

"He's working. Can I help you with something?"

The brunette stood...and that's when Nicki saw it—an infant carrier, the type that transferred from car to stroller, was tucked into the corner of the porch, away from the scorching sun, complete with bonneted baby inside.

"I'm really sorry to..." The brunette shook her head and turned to retrieve her baby. "I shouldn't have come. I'm sorry."

Nicki's gaze trailed from the adorable baby to the gorgeous mother. "You want to come in?" she asked against her better judgment. "Use the phone or grab a glass of water or something?"

"No, I don't want to impose. I didn't know he was... I'd hoped he'd be home for lunch, but—"

"He's working in West Palm Beach. He doesn't come home for lunch very often. I'm Nicki." She offered her right hand, but quickly snapped it back. The grime under her fingernails was downright embarrassing.

"Oh," the brunette said, her shoulders sagging, as if in relaxation. "Nicki. From Chicago, right?"

She nodded.

"You're the little girl from across the street." Barbie doll smiled. "I've heard so much about you. I'm Mandy."

Mandy. The woman Ty had once considered marrying. Just the luck *she'd* drop by on the day designated for Verna's sunroom. "Oh."

"I see you've heard a lot about me, too."

Nicki began to shake her head. "No, not—"

"I'm really not an ogre. I'm just trying to do what's best for Mia." She nodded toward the baby. "I'm sorry to bother you, but I thought if he saw her—"

"Pardon me?"

"It's plain as day when you see her eyes."

Nicki glanced into the carrier, met two sparkling, familiar blue eyes, and quickly looked away. Suddenly dizzy, she reached for the door handle, catching herself and preventing a stumble to the floor. "Are you saying—"

"I don't want to give him any trouble, you understand. I'm not looking for a husband. I just—"

"I think you'd better come in." Nicki felt her brow furrow and her head ache. She opened the door. "It's so hot, don't you want to sit down?"

Mandy flipped her perfect hair over a perfect shoulder and shifted the infant carrier from hand to perfect hand. "Maybe. It's almost time for her feeding, so...Thanks."

Nausea churned in Nicki's stomach, but she stepped aside and allowed her rival to enter.

"Looks like he's gotten a lot done. He always was a genius with this sort of thing."

Nicki nodded, inching toward the kitchen and biting back the urge to blab that most of the progress hadn't been Ty's handiwork, but her own. "Kitchen still isn't done."

"One step at a time, I suppose."

"I'll get you settled, but then if you'll excuse me for a moment, I should clean up. I've been working at Verna's, and—"

"Bless your heart." Mandy smiled, revealing perfect teeth. "That old bird drove me crazy."

Nicki selected a glass from a cabinet, filled it with ice and water, and left it on the makeshift counter for Mandy. "We have a shortage of chairs, but there's a chaise in the conservatory." She pointed in the general direction, hating the idea of another woman occupying the piece of furniture she'd come to think of as hers. "Do you need anything for...Mia, is it?"

"Yes, it's Mia. And thanks, but I come equipped with everything she needs right now." Another perfect smile.

And before a perfect breast popped out of Mandy's perfect, yellow lapel, Nicki made an exit, tears filling her eyes. None of it made sense, and she had so many questions she didn't know which to ask first. But she climbed the stairs, sorting through what she knew.

Beautiful Mandy had a gorgeous, blue-eyed baby—a baby she wanted Ty to see. And despite the fact Mandy wasn't looking for a husband, Ty had admitted he once considered marrying this woman.

She raced into the bathroom and splashed her dirt-streaked face with cold water. There had to be a logical explanation for what Mandy alluded to, but all signs pointed to one common thread in the whole mess. That baby had Ty's eyes—the resemblance *was* uncanny—and if what Mandy said was true, Ty was Mia's father.

*   *   *

Nicki wasn't answering her phone. Didn't she know he was dancing on top of the world? He was flying high, and there was no one with whom he'd rather share the elation. He gave his home number a try, grinning like a fish just off the hook. Custom Homebuilder of the Year. *Take that, Dad.*

"Hello?"

He pulled the phone from his ear and checked the ID screen. Sure enough, he'd dialed his home number, but he didn't recognize the voice.

"Hello?" she said again.

"Hi. Who is this?"

"Ty? Ty, it's Mandy."

In an instant, his heartbeat clamored in his ears, his tongue tasted like cotton, and bullets of sweat appeared at his temples. "Mandy?" He fell against Betty's driver side door, his hands clammy and his throat dry. "What are you doing at my place?"

"I brought Mia. I—"

"You brought the baby?"

"I thought if you saw her, you'd—"

"Where's Nicki?"

"She's... Why? She's upstairs. In the shower, I think, but—"

He mindlessly climbed into the car and, in a daze, turned the key. The car sputtered, but she started without subsequent attempts. *Thanks, Betty.* "You haven't talked to her, have you?"

"Well, of course I—"

"You have to go. Get out of there."

"I have rights, Ty. Mia has rights."

"And so do I, when it comes to my house."

"Listen, I only came because you've given me no other choice."

"No other choice? Mandy, I gave you a vial of my blood. If that baby's mine, prove it."

"I don't have to. I know in my heart."

"I'm calling my lawyer."

"Look at the baby. That's all I'm asking—that you see her."

"My lawyer will force the DNA test. You'll know the truth, we'll both know, in a week to ten days."

A dull silence answered him.

139

He sighed. "I think we both know the truth already, though, don't we?"

"She looks like you. You'd know that if you'd taken the time to—"

"Maybe I should've taken the time. Maybe I should've, and I'm sorry. I've done a lot of soul searching these past few weeks, and I'm the first to admit I have some growing to do. But, Mandy, if I ever meant anything to you, you'll go. Let the lawyers sort it out. Your being there is the worst possible—"

"What does that have to do with anything?"

"Promise me you'll go."

"Is it Nicki? Since when is she more than the little girl from across the street?"

"I'm on my way now. It would help if you weren't there when I got home."

"That's fine, Ty. When I'm finished feeding her—"

"Can't you feed her in the car?"

"I'm breast-feeding."

His fingers twitched against the steering wheel. Breast-feeding. Suddenly, and for the first time, he realized the baby was more than the object of a paternity suit. She was a nursing infant who probably kept her mother up at night. Maybe she cried a lot. Perhaps she smiled when sung to. He wondered if babies her age laughed, whether this one made pretty cooing noises. Was she healthy? Chubby? Did she snuggle herself to sleep?

"I'm sorry," Mandy said. "I'm sorry for all of this. But I wouldn't be doing it if I weren't ninety-nine percent sure."

"Neither would I."

She sighed. "She's yours, Ty. I'm sure."

"We'll see, won't we?"

CHAPTER 15

Nicki hurriedly twisted her wet hair into a clip and stepped into a red sundress. The rest of her clothes she stuffed haphazardly into her suitcases, the wrinkling of her garments far from being one of her worries.

With a suitcase in each hand, and the shoulder straps of both a garment bag and carry-on crisscrossed across her chest like ammunition belts, she walked quickly and quietly down the steps.

In the kitchen, the baby fussed, and with a perfect, soothing voice, Mandy calmed her. "Shh. It's all right, Li'l Mia."

Nicki shuffled out the door, tears clouding her sight, and turned northbound, toward Verna's house. She'd been a damn fool to think she belonged with Ty Carmichael.

"Nicki."

She stopped, pulled in a difficult, stuttering breath, and looked toward the voice, floating inland from the intracoastal.

"Can I give you a hand?" Tabor was climbing onto Ty's pier, tying his boat with a loose knot to a single post.

She began to shake her head, attempting to forage ahead, but when she hiked up her bags, the one in her left hand knocked those hanging across her chest, and in true domino effect, one hit led to another until she could no longer control their ricochets and sank into a sobbing heap among her cheap, red tapestry suitcases. She hid her face in her hands, willing the muscled egomaniac to disappear.

But within seconds, Tabor was on his haunches at her side, wearing too tight cut-off sweat shorts—and nothing else. The aroma of coconut suntan oil oozed from his bronze skin.

"I'm fine," Nicki said before he uttered a word. "I'm sure you have better things to do."

"Better things than helping a damsel in distress?"

"I'm not." She wiped tears from her moist cheeks, took a deep breath, and, finding her bearings, straightened her dress.

"In distress? Sure looks like it." He pulled two of her suitcases from her hands. "Where to?"

"I'm fine really. And your boat's drifting."

"Maybe I'll lose it." He smirked, pulling her up by the elbow. "I could use the insurance money for a new one anyway."

What a jerk.

"So where are we going with everything you own?"

"Number thirty-one. Two houses down."

"What do you say we unload all this, and I give you a real south Florida experience?"

"Let's get one thing straight," she said. "I can't begin to tell you what I've been through the past few months, and I wouldn't want to talk about it, if I could. I don't want to talk about anything, and your 'real south Florida experience' is at the top of that list. I'm not taking my clothes off for you—or anyone else, for that matter—and I don't care to know what's under your shorts. I appreciate your help, but it isn't going to get you anywhere, so decide right now whether you want to take another step."

His black eyes were as round as saucers, and his mouth hung slightly open in surprise. "I was just going to take you for a boat ride."

She sniffled and wiped more tears away. "Oh."

*   *   *

"Nicki?"

No answer.

"Nicki, I'm home."

Before he explored the echoing hallways of his home, he knew Nicki had gone. He'd promptly removed his dirty work boots upon entering and was dashing along the route to the kitchen, now a straight line without supplies creeping into the path along the way. She'd done a good job organizing his house, and an even better one straightening his head.

And all for nothing. That's what he had, now that she'd gone:

nothing. He entered the kitchen and stopped. Her graph paper sketches were taped to the walls, showing cabinetry in elevation. God, she was good at what she did. He'd always known that, of course, but perhaps he hadn't fully respected her talent, much in the same way he hadn't completely appreciated her as a woman, until he'd invited her, fully and completely, into his heart.

Her drawings showed she was as passionate about her work as she'd been, for a short while, about him. All he had left were memories. Memories of her smile, her scent. Memories of the day he'd dropped her to the kitchen floor. *Right here. This is where she stoked a fire that will rage until the day I die.*

And she was right. It did make more sense to keep the dishes near the sink.

He dialed her cell phone for the thirtieth time. When she again didn't answer, he called Verna. "Is she there?"

"Oh, sugar cube." Gum sounds popped through the receiver. "You've really made a mess of this, haven't you?"

"Guilty." He pinched the bridge of his nose. "Is she there?"

"No. But she was. Dropped every-flipping-thing she owned in my sunroom and cruised out the door faster than I could slip her a drink."

"But you have her stuff?"

"Honey, I got more of everyone else's stuff in this place than I do my own. Got to put George's out on the curb someday."

"So she's coming back. If you have her things, she's coming back."

"I don't know how to tell you this, so I'm just going to say it. She's out on the ocean with that jackass, Tabor."

His stomach churned with the thought of his sweetheart in the company of such a sleaze. "But that means she's coming back."

"I reckon."

"Could you call me when she gets there?"

"Will do. Love ya, hon. Hang in there."

"Thanks."

Waiting would be purgatory, but he supposed he deserved the torture. He slipped through what would someday be a serving pantry, through the dining room, avoiding the conservatory. He passed through the front room, where she'd neatly laid out his tools and stacked his supplies, and then he climbed the stairs.

She'd obviously left in a hurry. Her body wash still occupied a shelf in the shower, along with a pink razor, and next to an abandoned lipstick in his medicine cabinet was a velvet ring box.

He held his breath as he opened the box. "Damn it." She'd returned the ring. Didn't she know she was meant to wear it? Didn't she realize they'd work through this?

His closet seemed empty without her clothes hanging, according to color, along the racks, and the four laundry baskets she'd positioned at the far end of the closet for sorting—lights, darks, towels, and hand-washables—were void of her garments, save a pair of tiny pink panties. He pulled his sketch books from the shelf and, knowing he couldn't avoid the room forever, followed his heart strings to the conservatory.

He stood near the windows, staring out at the waterway. When he opened his sketchbook, he began to wander aimlessly throughout the room. A wrenching knot plummeted through his chest when he flipped to the page boasting Nicki's gorgeous figure sprawled on the chaise longue. Without realizing he'd done so, he'd lowered his body to the very piece of furniture, feeling numb.

Perhaps it was the vague scent of raspberries, vanilla, and roses that alerted him. Maybe it was the worn, pink velour beneath his fingers. Whatever it was that caught his attention captured him so completely that a tingling, aching sensation filtered through him. This room would always be special because of what had happened here.

Flashes of her body fought their way into his mind. Ring on the fourth left toe. Beauty mark on the left cheek of her rear. Bruise-darkened spine.

Bruised wrist, bruised hip.

Bruised heart.

He'd hurt her, and that hurt most of all. Sorrow boiled to anger, and he sprang up, sending the sketch book tumbling to the floor. He darted into the kitchen, pacing restlessly from one end of the half-assembled room to the other.

A sledge hammer, that's what he needed. He turned around to retrieve it, but, that's right, she'd moved it. *Where'd she put it? Where was it?* With the tools, on the other side of the god-damned house in the front room. One of the only rooms he hadn't gutted. One of the only rooms he didn't need to use it in. What a pain in the ass to walk all the way in there to find it. He yanked it from the makeshift table, sending a screwdriver spiraling to the floor with a *clank, clank, clink.*

The sledge hammer was as heavy as his heart. He bobbed it in the air, testing its weight in his arms. "Screw it." He swung the hammer into the plaster and shattered the front room wall as easily as he'd destroyed Nicki's trust.

*   *   *

Tabor didn't talk to her. If he did, she didn't hear him over the hum of the boat motor, and that was just as well. She leaned against the vinyl cushioned seat on the port side and stared out over the ocean. Such a vast, blue unknown. Not unlike Ty Carmichael's eyes. A broken sigh escaped with her next breath, spurring a new welling of tears.

Oh, for heaven's sake, stop already. She brushed them away with her fingertips.

Parasailing tourists braved the skies above her, and snorkeling vacationers swam the waters below. What made their lives so easy? Or was she making life too difficult?

Perhaps she'd been too hasty in departing. She hadn't heard Ty's side of the story after all. But it wasn't the possibility of a baby that bothered her; it was the fact he'd hidden it. If he'd told her months ago, weeks ago, even days ago, about Mia, things might have been different. His silence regarding the matter meant either he wasn't owning up to the responsibility of fatherhood, or he didn't feel strongly enough about her to share such news.

Well, she knew what it was like to grow up without a father, and she didn't wish it on any baby girl. And she wasn't about to pursue a relationship with a man who wasn't as committed to her as she was to him.

*   *   *

Well, what did he have to lose? He couldn't just sit there, covered in plaster dust, waiting for his life to fall in line. After all, he was in this pickle because he'd refused to take control of his future.

Had he been proactive—hell, had he been active, period—he could have filed a countersuit against Mandy, forcing her to gather DNA through amniocentesis. If he wasn't the baby's father, he would have saved himself a world of worry. And if he was, he would have told Nicki months ago.

Loose ends. His whole damn life had begun to fray when he'd left Chicago, and he'd better do something about it now to get back on track. He picked up the phone and dialed. 1. 7-7-3... And before he could change his mind, he punched in the remaining seven digits.

Predictably, on the third ring, he heard Ruth Anne Carmichael's subdued hello.

"Hi, Mom." A dreaded silence. "It's me. Ty. How are things? How are you?"

"Ty?"

"Yeah. Hi."

A whimper, or maybe a laugh, sounded through the phone. "Hello, Ty."

He released a held breath. "Hi."

"Are you all right?"

"Yeah. No. Kind of."

"I've wanted to call. Christmas, your birthday...I hate to think of you alone..."

"Why don't we start with today? With now?"

After a few moments, she spoke again. "Your father heard a rumor today."

A weary smile broke through, and he brushed his thumb against a callus on his forefinger.

"Custom Homebuilder of the Year," she said. "And your name was mentioned."

"It was my project."

"Congratulations, Tyler."

"I have so much to tell you."

"Freddi's just signed a two-million-dollar renovation in Lake Forest, and Krissy's made sous-chef in—"

"I don't want to talk about the twins." He shook his head. "I found someone, Mom. A girl. More than worthy of Aunt Evie's ring."

"When?"

"So many years ago."

"Years? And you're just now calling?"

"It's just...well....I think I just lost her. Got a minute?"

And he proceeded to tell his mother everything.

*   *   *

Nicki disembarked from Tabor's boat with a polite thank you and a small wave. The sun had nearly set and the air had turned cool, leaving her to briskly rub her suntanned arms from shoulders to elbows, hoping for a spark of warmth.

She saw Ty immediately, illuminated by the light of a single pillar candle on the bistro table in the garden. He was still in work clothes, which made him even more irresistible, and his hair curled out from beneath his Chicago Bulls Three-peat hat, which he wore backwards. His forehead rested in one hand, and a bottle of beer hung from the other. She stopped and stared, her heart begging her to give him another chance. Surely, someone as amazing as Ty deserved an opportunity to explain.

Tears again crept into her eyes, convincing her to duck through the garden gate, to hightail it to Verna's house before she caved, and before he saw her. But two steps into her plan, he spoke.

"What are you doing out on the ocean with that guy?" When he looked up, his gaze, with eyes somehow shining through the dusk, seemed to pierce hers, as if he'd known of her hesitance and her position on the lawn all along.

She crossed her arms over her breasts, hiding her chilled nipples peeking through the snuggly-fitting, cotton dress. "What do you care?" She started toward the gate.

"I know I hurt you."

"Do you?" She spun toward him again.

"But being angry with me is no reason put yourself in danger. You don't know that man from Adam."

"I fail to see how this is any business of yours."

"You know how I feel about that idiot."

"How do you feel about me?"

"You know how I feel about you."

"I thought I did."

"Regardless, while you're here, I'm responsible for you, and sailing off into the ocean with—"

"You want to be responsible, Ty? Be responsible for your daughter." She again began toward Verna's house.

"Wait." He plunged into her path.

*   *   *

She glared at him, but he stood firm, cautiously reaching for her. "I love you, Nicki."

She shook away from him, tears sprouting full force. "Shut up, shut up, shut up! I'm tired of hearing that from men who don't deserve to say it."

"Let me explain."

"I have to go."

"Where are you going?"

"Verna's."

"Verna's place is a mess. It'll drive you crazy, staying there."

"What does that tell you?"

So she'd rather wade through a collection of batiks, yin yang, and incense, not to mention dealing with a dead husband who may or may not appear, than look at him.

"I won't be there for long anyway. I'm going back to Chicago."

"When?" It came out in a hushed whisper.

"I don't know. Tomorrow morning. Earliest possible flight."

Her news cut like a knife, and when she walked around him, he was powerless to stop her. She hit the flagstone path, and the clapping of her sandals rose into the evening air and reverberated in his heart. "Nicki, wait."

His words were quieter than he'd intended. Maybe she hadn't heard him, maybe she chose not to respond, but she continued to walk. He pulled his cell phone from his pocket.

The clicking of her shoes ceased when her phone rang. He watched as she lifted the flap of her tiny shoulder bag, pulled out her phone, and put it to her ear. "I can't talk to you," she whispered.

"You can always talk to me."

"Not this time."

"Then listen. Just listen."

She sighed, hanging her head like scorned child's. *Click, click* tapped her toes against the stones. "I'm listening."

"I wanted to tell you. I was going to."

"When? Next month? Next year? You still haven't said a damn word about it."

"Mandy was here. You already know."

"I want you to say it. My God, Ty." She sobbed. "Extend me that courtesy, at least."

He took a deep breath. "Nicki."

"Say it, or I'm walking."

"I might be a father." His lack of hesitation surprised him. If he'd known it would have been that easy to say, he would have told her ages ago. "But I don't think it's possible."

"She has your eyes."

"Yeah, well, a lot of people have blue eyes."

"Have you seen her yet?" Slowly, she turned around, tears staining her pink cheeks.

"No."

"Ty, she's beautiful."

"I'm sure she is." He ended the call, slipped the phone back into his pocket, and took a step toward her. "But I don't think she's mine."

"Why not?"

"The dates are wrong."

"When did you last...spend time...with her mother?"

"Last fall. Late October, early November."

"Well, that's precise."

"It was at least four weeks earlier than it would have to be for the baby to be mine. Well, two weeks anyway. She was early."

"Let me give you some advice. Stop talking. You're burying yourself."

"I'm safe, Nicki. I'm always safe."

"The way you are with me?"

He sighed, pulled the cap off, and shoved his fingers through his hair. "You agreed to wear my ring, for God's sake." He tucked the hat back on his head. "That was the night I asked you to spend the rest of your life with me, Nicki."

"If there was one night with me, there was probably one night with her."

"I could question your rule about artists, if you want to play that game. You slept with one, and he happened to be me, right?"

"That's the difference between you and me." She wiped away another tear. "I don't play games."

He sighed, able only to look at her...unable to speak.

"I can't believe you'd say that," she whispered.

Neither could he.

"So tell me, Ty, if I call in two weeks to tell you I'm late, possibly pregnant, are you going to turn your back on me, too?"

"I couldn't do that, Nicki."

"Well, you're doing it to someone." She wrapped her arms around her body.

"You're cold."

"And I'm tired, and I'm scared, and I've never felt this alone my entire life. That doesn't mean I want your body anywhere near mine right now."

He touched the cold flesh of her upper arm, and she didn't flinch or pull away. Instead, she rolled her tear-filled eyes and leaned into him.

"If I had told you," he asked, "do you think we'd have happened?"

Slowly, she raised her eyes and shook her head. "I don't know."

"Then I'm not sorry." He wrapped his arms around her lovely body. "I'd prefer to have you forever, but between a few short months and never, there's no contest. How can I be sorry for the chance to love you?"

"Aren't you sorry for Mandy? For Mia? That's her name, you know. Mia."

"My lawyer told me."

"Lawyer?"

"For the paternity suit."

She pressed her hands against his chest. "There's a paternity suit?"

Oh, hell. Something else she didn't know.

"Don't you think she'd have to be fairly certain to file a paternity suit?"

He opened his mouth to answer, but she didn't give him the chance.

"Do me a favor," she said. "Tonight, while you're basking in the comfort of your queen-sized bed, with no one there to throw a knee between your legs, consider how you've always felt about the man who left my mother, six months pregnant with the rent due. Consider how you've always felt about the man who had better things to do than be my father. And then remember you might be that man right now for another single mother, another fatherless child."

"Nicki."

"You once searched exhaustively for my father. Maybe you can find Mia's in the mirror."

He tightened his grip and lowered his forehead to hers. "I don't think she's mine."

"But you don't know, do you? She might be your daughter, and you're turning your back on her. I love you, Ty, but I can't accept that. I'm sorry, but I can't." She pulled away from him.

He nodded, pretending to understand, but he didn't. Why couldn't she realize they had something special? That they could outlast anything?

"Before I go, I want to thank you for everything you've done for me. Not just the past few months, making me feel like a woman again. But before, when I was a little girl. Making me feel human. I won't forget it."

"Don't make me follow you back to Chicago, Nicki."

"You belong here, bright eyes. There may be a little girl who needs you here."

He lifted her chin and stared into her eyes, remembering the little girl who had needed him in Chicago. That little girl was gone now, grown into a strong woman. And like it or not, she didn't need anyone.

CHAPTER 16

"Are you sure I can't convince you to stay, pumpkin spice?" Verna was a ball of energy at five in the morning, leaning over the teal countertop, shoving a cup of herbal tea into Nicki's hands.

Nicki shook her head. "I have so much to do. Apologize profusely to my roommate, grovel at my mother's feet, hope the Institute has a few openings for fall semester."

"Ten to one, it ain't the to-do list that's ailing you." She drummed her fingernails, one broken in a jagged slant, against the countertop.

"Of course it isn't. But I'm doing the right thing."

Verna shrugged. "Time will tell, my little sweet pea. Time will tell. You just take that time, and use it wisely, hear? Don't make this decision right now, and if you have to decide something, decide to do nothing. It's still a decision, and you still made it."

Nicki sipped her tea. "You know what I did last night when I couldn't sleep? I tried to remember what it was like to sleep without him, and I couldn't. And even if I could, I don't know how I'm going to wake up tomorrow."

"Oh, honey, you just do it. We all do. And before you know it, going to sleep ain't so hard neither. You go to sleep, you wake up, you miss him from time to time. You'll remember the good times and you'll want to have more. And you will. You're too young not to. You'll remember he loves you, even though he hurt you. And eventually, you'll realize you probably hurt him, too. It ain't fair. It ain't pretty. But that's the way the horsies gallop around this nutty carousel."

Nicki nodded, leaned back in her chair, and stretched her aching arms above her head. Her whole body hurt, and every muscle was tired. But she didn't expect to sleep anytime soon. Too much on her mind, too many unanswered questions. She yawned.

"And if it's all worth it," Verna said, "if he's your soul mate, you'll find a way to be together forever. I know you don't believe that right now, but it'll happen if it's supposed to."

Nicki looked to her cup of tea, but out of the corner of her eye, she caught sight of a moving figure in the sunroom and quickly turned back toward it. There was nothing there, but she could have sworn…

"Did you see him that time?" Verna grinned.

*   *   *

At dawn, Ty leaned against the square newel post on his front porch, watching Nicki step into a taxi in front of Verna's house. He hoped she'd stop to say goodbye.

But she didn't. When the cab slowed at his driveway, she touched her lips with the tips of her fingers, blew him a kiss, and mouthed three significant words. But then she was gone, leaving him waving like a romantic fool.

He'd done as she'd asked. He'd thought long and hard about Mandy's position, about the role he may or may not have played in putting her there. He sympathized, something he hadn't done since the day Mandy called with the news. *Ty, I'm pregnant.* He wasn't about to take responsibility then for something he hadn't done. And while he wanted Mia to have a father now, he wouldn't be a stand-in.

On the other hand, if he was wrong, he'd missed so much. The entire pregnancy, the birth, the first few weeks. According to his mother—who'd been matter-of-fact about the possibility of being a grandmother, neither excited nor disappointed—babies didn't smile until about five or six weeks. He didn't want to miss her first toothless grin. He'd missed her first breath, her first feeding, her first bath. Just in case he was wrong, he wasn't going to miss anything else.

Despite the early hour, he dialed Mandy's cell phone number before he lost the nerve.

"Ty? It's six in the morning."

"I'm sorry for calling so early."

"I'm surprised you're calling at all."

"Yeah, well, Nicki opened my eyes to something. Besides, I figured

152

you'd probably be up with your daughter. Babies are always up early, aren't they?"

"Not when they don't sleep at night."

"Oh, so I probably woke you, didn't I? I'm sorry, but I was wondering. What sort of visitation schedule would you be proposing?"

"Excuse me?"

"I'm not saying she's mine, but I'm not saying she isn't either. If she were, when would I see her?"

"When would you want to see her?"

"I don't know. A night during the week, maybe one night a weekend. I guess whatever's standard."

"We can work something out."

"Can I take her this Friday? You're staying with your parents now, right? I can be to their place around four."

"Why don't I meet you instead and we can talk about things. Your place isn't baby-ready, you know, and neither is your car. Do you even have seat belts?"

He hadn't thought about that. "No. Where do you want to meet?"

"How about that charming café on Alhambra? The three of us can have dinner."

The Casablanca Café. The first place he'd taken Nicki. No way. "How about something a little less formal? Like a park or something?"

"That's fine, too, I guess."

"So, this may be coming too late, but tell me about it. What time of day was she born? How was it?"

"You want to know? Now?"

"Yeah. What was it like? How big is she? Did she cry right away? I guess we could talk Friday, but—"

"I was induced at eight in the morning on March fourteenth, and my sister was in the delivery room…"

CHAPTER 17

Nicki dropped her robe and climbed onto the pedestal at the hub of Studio C. Twelve hundred miles away, her breasts, cast in chocolate, were on display at Las Olas Art Center. And it probably wasn't raining in Fort Lauderdale.

She held her position, staring into the dark beyond the students and counting the minutes until the session would come to a close. She was merely a body. A body artists captured on paper, but didn't think about again.

And it would soon be that way with Ty. Eventually, they'd both recover from the pain inflicted on the Isle of Venice, and inevitably, they'd move on in separate directions.

The air in the studio was cool and smelled of the clay thrown onto pottery wheels in the classroom next door. The walls were gray, the floor was gray, and beyond the windows of the Art Institute, even the palette of Chicago's sky was gray. She closed her eyes and breathed deeply, reaching for the memory of an intracoastal breeze.

Ah, there it is. Warm, balmy. Jasmine and ocean. And he's there, too. A trace of peppermint. Hard work and muscle. Callused hands, bright eyes. Flirty, irresistible half-smile. She didn't want to open her eyes. It would all fade when she did.

Her eyes filled with tears and she snapped them open, forcing herself to face her own reality, however mundane and lonely.

Long minutes later, students began to gather their supplies, and one by one, they disappeared into the hall. She covered her body and

154

headed toward the small compartment in the back of the room where her clothing hung in a locker.

She dressed and headed out into the dreary city. She boarded a Chicago Transit Authority bus and sank against the cold, cracked vinyl seat. The vehicle smelled of stale crackers and humus. So different than the water taxis of Fort Lauderdale, perfumed with salty sea air and south Florida earth.

She pulled out her cell phone and made a much overdue phone call. "Hi, Mom." Her half-brothers shrieked in the background.

"I'm not even going to talk to you, unless you tell me you're back home."

"Yeah. I got in a couple weeks ago."

"Good. I'll call you soon, okay? The baby came down with a nasty cold yesterday, and I can't get a moment's peace."

"I was hoping we could—"

"And we will. Soon." One of the monsters screamed even louder. "Tomorrow, maybe, okay?"

"Okay."

"Bye."

Nicki stared out the window, attempting to envision Ty on Chicago sidewalks. She couldn't form the picture in her mind. He no longer belonged there, and deep down, she knew she didn't either. But unlike him, she didn't have the wherewithal to take flight and start over.

She longed to escape, to choose a destination solely because it reminded her of a peaceful time and place, the way Fort Lauderdale brought Ty back to inland waterways in Italy. But she hadn't been anywhere, and even if she had, nothing could compare to the Isle of Venice. Or the company she'd found there.

When she reached her building, a man clad in a black overcoat and tasseled shoes opened the vestibule door from the inside, allowing her to enter. She didn't want to talk to anyone. She didn't want to smile. She wanted nothing more than to wash the studio and the city from her skin and indulge in some much-needed sleep.

"Thanks," she said, not bothering to make eye contact.

"You're welcome, Nicolette." The voice was deep, clear, and familiar. And few people called her Nicolette.

She turned toward him, her key halfway into the main door's lock, and met the blue eyes of Ty's father. She'd never noticed it before, but his eyes were bright, too. Just like Ty's.

"I couldn't find your number at the office, and you're unlisted, which is good for a single girl in the city," he said.

Like father, like son. Didn't either of them have anything better to do than lecture her about safety?

"You never know what might happen. I'm glad you realize that. But it means I have to drop by unannounced."

"Did Ty send you?"

"No, Ruth Anne did. Want to grab a sandwich and a cup of coffee?"

Too intrigued to refuse, which is what she really wanted to do, she nodded, and without a word, she accompanied him to the diner across the street.

Once seated at a booth too worn for the likes of Robert Carmichael's suit, he pulled a rolled magazine from the inside pocket of his overcoat and slid it across the table. "I assume you know about this."

She smiled upon catching sight of the Jewel Box and shook her head. "No, I—"

"Page seventeen."

She flipped pages, and there it was in black and white: "A Cut Above the Rest: Diamond Custom Homes, Custom Homebuilder of the Year. Architectural design and rough carpentry headed by Ty Carmichael. Interior design by Nicolette Paige."

She smiled. He'd done it. And he deserved it. But when she looked back to his father, she sobered. "Robert, he's good at what he does."

He drummed his fingers on the tabletop. "As evidenced by the experts."

She raised an eyebrow. "You're an expert."

"Ruth Anne's planned a trip a week from Friday."

"Book a hotel room. He has four bedrooms, but three are in pieces. It'll drive you crazy staying there."

"Oh, I'm not going. But you are."

"I don't think I—"

"As we speak, my secretary is filing a letter of commendation with the Building Commissioner of Broward County on your behalf."

Her jaw fell open, but she quickly drew it closed.

"You know I've just come back, right? You know things didn't end well."

Robert pulled a pen and notepad from the inside pocket of his jacket and began scribbling. "This is the number of the company that moved Krissy to France. They're expecting your call. And here's your flight information. Your ticket will be waiting for you at check-in."

"I can't go. There's more than that damn letter of commendation keeping me here, Robert, or rather, keeping me from him. There's...so much more. I can't begin to tell you."

"You'll have a full four days before my wife arrives to straighten it out." He clicked his pen closed and slid the notepad across the table.

"Does he know about this? What you're doing for me?"

"Ruth Anne thought it best not to tell him until you agreed."

"Things happened long before I set foot in south Florida, and he needs to own up to those things. If I go, I give him reason—"

"I assume you're talking about this baby."

"He told you about Mia."

"No, he told Ruth Anne. He also told her he complied with the court order for DNA testing weeks ago, while you were there, so with or without you in his life, he's willing to—"

"I beg your pardon?"

"He submitted a sample for DNA testing."

Why hadn't he told her? "Well, if he's ready to do the right thing, how do you know he'll want me there at all? You haven't so much as talked to him."

Robert's glance hardened. "How long has it been since you've known how he feels about you? A few months? I've known for years. There's no doubt in my mind."

"Years?"

"You're a good designer, Nicolette. Do you see any reason I'd withhold a letter of commendation for a designer of your magnitude, other than needing a way to reach my son?"

"I beg your pardon?"

He opened a menu. "With that letter, you shouldn't have any trouble finding a job in Fort Lauderdale. I'll get you a copy for your records."

She massaged her temples. "Back up. You used me to reach Ty?"

"I didn't use anything more than your natural ability to design, and I paid you handsomely for it, considering your status as an intern. But yes, I withheld your letter with an ulterior motive."

"Explain."

"Had I written that letter, you'd be designing in some posh showroom on Michigan Avenue or somewhere on the North Shore. You'd have had no reason to turn to Ty, and that's what you needed to do. Of course, I didn't expect your fiancé or this baby, but—"

"And why did I need to turn to Ty?"

"Isn't it obvious? The two of you together...well, here it is." He tapped a finger against the *Custom Home* headline. "You're a stunning team."

She watched him study the menu, wanting to verbally slice him to pieces. She wasn't his child, and she certainly was no longer his employee. He'd done a wonderful thing in writing the long overdue letter of commendation for her and arranging for her return to Florida, but he couldn't tell her what to do, couldn't decide this for her the way he'd orchestrated important events in the lives of his children.

And then it hit her. "I understand," she said. "You didn't do this for me. You did it all for Ty."

"For both of you." He nodded. "And for Ruth Anne. How's the soup here?"

"It's fine." She shook her head, confused by his nonchalance, angered with his using her to reach his son. But at the same time, she felt a warm sense of gratitude for all he'd done. He'd lain a path, she'd followed, and as a result, Ty had succeeded.

"What are you going to have?" Robert asked from behind his menu.

He didn't expect her to think about food right now, did he? "I don't know."

At last, he looked at her. "You're like a daughter to me, always have been. So I've been hard on you. Take it as a compliment. I'm hard on all my children."

"You're rationalizing."

"But it's true. You were probably no happier seeing me in your doorway than you'd be seeing your ex-fiancé, and maybe you want flush my offer down the toilet. But, Nicolette, don't make my son pay for a mistake I made. What's your first instinct? Do you want to go?"

"Yes," she said without thinking.

"Then you're going."

A wheel turned in her head. She could use Robert's rationale against him. "On one condition."

"I'm impressed." A small smile appeared in his eyes. "A negotiation."

"When Ruth Anne arrives on Friday, you're with her."

He began to shake his head.

"Then my answer is no. If you want to make amends with your son, if you want to make his life better by placing me back in it, you'll do more than pull strings. I won't go without the promise that you'll be there, too."

Robert folded his menu and set it aside. "I think I'll try the clam chowder and a B.L.T."

*   *   *

"What a beautiful baby."

It was the third time in no more than ten minutes he'd heard the comment from passersby, and Ty nodded at the old, blue-haired woman beside Mandy. "Thanks."

His ex-girlfriend had packed a picnic dinner and multitudes of baby supplies for their visit at Sunset Lake. Mia, dressed in a white cotton dress that looked handmade, stared up at him from a pink-and-yellow plaid bouncer.

"Let's see," the old woman said, peering closer. "I think she looks like her daddy."

Ty stretched his legs on the blanket Mandy was thoughtful enough to bring and nodded. "Popular opinion."

"You still don't see it?" Mandy asked when the woman had walked on. She unclipped the safety harness that held the baby in place and lifted her out of the seat. "Look at her, Ty. Really look this time."

Before he knew what was happening, Mia was wiggling and fussing in his arms. "I can't..." He shifted her from arm to arm. "I don't know how to do this."

"You're doing fine."

"Doubtful." He rested the baby on her back against his thighs and stared at her as she cried. So she had blue eyes. It was a coincidence they were as unusually bright as his. "She's beautiful, Mandy. She's a pretty little girl."

Images of another pretty little girl flashed in his head, and he bit his lip to prevent a desperate sigh. "But she's just a few weeks old. She doesn't look like me any more than she looks like you. She looks like a baby. She looks like herself." He gently bounced his knees, and her cries downgraded to sniffling.

"She looks like you. Can't you open your mind to the possibility?"

"I'm trying. Not for your sake, not for mine. For hers. But I'm sorry, I don't feel it." Mia gripped his thumb, and the sigh finally escaped him. "It's breaking my heart, but I don't."

Mandy turned to a picnic basket and began to sort through it. "Maybe it's going to take some time."

He nodded, wondering how long it had taken his father to feel a connection, whether he was still waiting to feel it. "There's something you should know."

She raised her brows, but didn't take her eyes from the sandwiches, peaches, and celery sticks she doled onto paper plates.

"I'm going to be a terrible father."

"No, you aren't."

Mia began to fuss again, and he brought her to his shoulder, gently patting her back. "Yes, I am. I don't know how to do this. I've been holding her for half a minute, and I can't wait for you to stop what you're doing and take her back. I don't know how to hold her, how to talk to her, and God, I hope I never have to change a diaper because it might take me all night."

"Give it some time."

"My father—lousy father. My grandfather—I don't think I ever saw him, even though he lived across town, so he was probably worse. I have no example to follow, and as far as instinct goes—"

"Don't look now, but you're proving yourself wrong."

The baby's head rested against his shoulder, and his cheek brushed against her feather-soft hair. She smelled of talcum and lavender. But no matter how badly he wanted to love her, he simply didn't feel it. He slowly pulled her from his shoulder and placed her back into the bouncer.

"I want to be wrong about this," he said. "I wish she were mine. I mean, look at her—she's beautiful. But I don't think it's possible."

"Stop thinking about yourself. Think about Mia."

"I am thinking about Mia. What happens when I've seen her a few times, we're attached and comfortable together, and then we find out she isn't mine?"

"You can see her whenever you want to see her, Ty, and before the thought enters your head, this isn't about you and me. I'm not using my daughter to keep you. But if you're right, if she isn't yours, you can still see her when you want to see her."

"I don't think I can do that, Mandy." He turned away and stared out over Sunset Lake.

*   *   *

In the confines of her small apartment, Nicki filled a plastic watering can, pushed the speaker-phone button on her cordless receiver, and dialed her voicemail. "You have one message," the computerized voice said.

"Nicki. Greetings from the intracoastal." She stopped watering a wilted Devil's Ivy mid-pour. A deep sigh resonated through the receiver, and her skin tingled with anticipation, desire. "I want to thank you for sharing your life with me, the past sixteen years of it, anyway, and I guess I wanted to say I'm sorry I lost the next sixty." A few quiet moments followed.

She sank against the countertop in her tiny kitchen, dropped the watering can into the sink, and reached for the receiver, staring down at it, as if her wishing could spring the real-life Ty Carmichael from its innards.

"Anyway, you don't need this. I'll try not to call, if that's what you want. I love you. I hope you know that."

She wiped tears from her eyes and turned off the phone, tapping the antenna against her bottom lip. His message played in her mind over and over again, along with every word he'd uttered in Florida. She closed her eyes and imagined his arms around her, his lips at her neck.

And suddenly, beauty pulsed within her, coinciding with every beat of her heart—the same sensation she felt while posing—and at once, she knew what she had to do to feel that way forever.

161

CHAPTER 18

"I really appreciate you coming straight from work," Verna said. "I know you're probably beat like a rug."

"No sense in going home," Ty said from his post atop a step ladder, where he was edging the ceiling of Verna's sunroom with white paint. "No one to go home to."

"Not yet anyway."

"And I'm tired after a long day in the field, but I can't sleep. I spend my evenings staring at Nicki's body parts cast in chocolate at the art center, and nights working on my own project. You should see the progress I've made on my place."

"I'll come by your place some time."

"Some time? Why not tonight?"

"You've got lots going on tonight." Verna nodded toward a manila envelope sitting upon a pile of George's old, dusty sport coats. "Everything's right there, huh? All of it."

Ty nodded. "Yeah, I had to go to the post office to sign for it when I got home from work."

"Ain't you going to open it?"

He shrugged. "Of course I'm going to open it. I just...I need to take my time. That envelope is a bomb, one way or another." He turned the bill of his Chicago Bulls hat to the back of his head. "How long has it been since you painted this ceiling?"

"Me, personally? I don't take stock in projects that don't show improvement."

"It's soaking up the paint like a sponge. It might need two coats."

Verna's many bracelets jangled when she waved a hand at him. "No use in painting the damn ceiling."

"Trust me, it'll look nice and fresh when we're done. Are you sure I can't talk you into a more subdued yellow? What you've got is a little too...shall we say flamboyant?"

"Honeysuckle, you can do whatever your little heart desires, so long as it involves lots and lots of yellow. That ugly son of a bitch is starting to hide things on me." She made a fist and looked down. "George, you can hide your willie-nillie in the devil's backside, for all I care, but so help me, quit taking my crochet hooks."

Ty smiled and shook his head.

"Come to think of it, blueberry pie—" She thrust the envelope toward him. "—you'd better take this before he hides this, too."

He climbed down from the ladder and took it. "My whole future's in this envelope. Am I a dad? Am I not? Did I lose Nicki for nothing? It's all in here. I'm scared to death to find out."

She chomped on pink bubble gum. "You been seeing that baby, right?"

"A couple times, yeah."

"What's your heart to have to say?"

He shrugged. "I don't know. I want her to be mine. For so many reasons, Verna, I want her to be mine, but she isn't. I don't feel it. I wish I did, but I don't. It's the strangest feeling. I'm so close to losing something I didn't know I wanted. And that's why I haven't opened that envelope. I know what it's going to say."

"Oh, baby cakes." Verna opened her arms and embraced him. "If your heart is right, and she ain't your little girl, don't you worry. You're going to be a fine daddy to someone someday."

He nodded. "And you've been a fine mother to me these past couple years."

"I tell you, I can be paid not to repeat that when your own mama comes to town."

He smiled, dropped to the floor, and grabbed a bottle of beer. "I still can't believe she's coming. And what's more, she's bringing my dad."

"Hhhmmm. How do you think that came to be?"

He shrugged, sipping the beer. "I don't know. One day, she said it was hopeless, and the next, she said he'd changed his mind."

"I'll bet you're excited."

"Nervous is more like it. It's been a long time."

She nodded. "Talk to Nicki lately?"

"No. She'll come to me when—or maybe I should say if—she's ready."

"You really love her, don't you?"

He looked down at his bottle. "Always have."

*   *   *

Nicki opened Ty's unlocked door and quickly shoved her suitcases inside. The rest of her belongings would be arriving in two days, courtesy of Robert Carmichael's bankbook.

She smiled, breathing in the comforting scent of drywall and plywood. *Home at last.*

First things first. How much time did she have? Verna said she'd keep Ty until seven. That gave her just under two hours to straighten up, start the spaghetti sauce, unpack, and shower. She could do it, providing Ty hadn't done too much damage in the weeks she'd been gone.

Just the opposite it turned out. With the exception of a new hole in one of the front room walls, it looked as though he'd been putting things back together. He'd painted the powder room beneath the stairs.

What's more, he'd finally taped and sanded the drywall in the kitchen, and he'd drawn, in indelible ink, the lines where the cabinetry would sit. Paint chips of pale yellow and pear green hung on the walls next to the cherry color sample she'd borrowed from the furniture store at the Galleria. So he was going to take her advice. He was going to use a painted and glazed finish on the perimeter cabinetry.

She opened a cabinet door and saw Verna had left the fixings for a spaghetti dinner. Nicki wished she'd had time for something more exotic, but spaghetti would have to suffice. With little time to spare, she went straight to work, chopping tomatoes, onions, and garlic.

When the sauce was simmering, she lugged her bags up the stairs. She gasped when she entered the master bedroom. Not because it was a disaster of strewn laundry, but because he'd finished and framed the drawing of her on the chaise longue and hung it above the unmade bed. She climbed onto the mattress among twisted linens for a closer look.

"Do I really look like that?" she whispered. Her fingers traced the curves of her figure on paper.

She'd never seen herself as beautiful as Ty had made her on paper. Maybe because she *wasn't*, and she'd seen plenty of artists' renditions to prove it. But if that's what Ty had captured, that's the way he felt about her. And the more and more she studied his work, the more of herself she saw in it. He'd found beauty in her every imperfection. Even her wide hips looked attractive and provocative. And suddenly, she wanted to see every drawing of her that he'd done in their time together.

What else does he see in me?

She scrambled to the closet, but his sketchbooks were not on their designated shelf. She blew a curl out of her eyes and drummed her fingers against the empty shelf, thinking. Where had he moved them?

Old habits died hard. They were hiding under the bed, as if he'd been studying them every night before falling asleep. She flipped one open to find he'd been doing more than looking at them; he'd been drawing her across twelve hundred miles.

He'd drawn her tumbled in the garden, reaching for the sun on the beach, laying across the hood his car. He'd recorded memories of her in the shower, memories of her catching snowflakes on State Street. He'd sketched things that had yet to happen: her sipping tea in the finished breakfast room, her leaning against the newel post of the front porch with a swollen, pregnant belly.

"He loves me," she whispered.

The phone rang and she stretched to reach it without abandoning the sketch book.

"Hey, raindrop, it's Verna."

"Hi. Is he on his way already?"

"No, he went to the hardware store to tone down my yellow, but then we're done for the night. My guess is you have about half an hour."

"Thanks."

"Welcome back."

Nicki smiled.

*   *   *

With his skin flecked with white ceiling paint, Ty opened his front door and instantly backed onto the porch to check the numbers on his mailbox. Number twenty-five Isle of Venice Drive. Sure enough, this was his home. And...he sniffed. And, yes, it smelled like tomato sauce.

The sound of running water filtered down the hallway, and half a moment later, a brilliant alto echoed through the walls. "Nicki?"

Her reply consisted of nothing more than the next verse of his shower song. With a hope as deep as the Atlantic, he bolted up the stairs. He'd recognize that voice anywhere, but it didn't make sense. He'd left her a message days ago; he hadn't heard word one in response. And now she was singing, presumably naked, in his shower.

His bed was made, his underwear drawer organized, and when he opened another drawer, the familiar, comforting scent of a rose sachet wafted about him. She was back, and if the empty velvet ring box were any indication, she was ready and willing to deal with whatever lay in their path. He smiled, took a tentative step toward the open bathroom door.

Her voice reverberated from the tub. And so thoughtfully, she'd put a Betty Boop soap dispenser on his vanity. He quietly stripped off his paint-splattered clothing, placed the loaded manila envelope atop the pile, and joined in singing the chorus, stepping into the tub next to her.

She froze, hands stationed among suds in her hair, opened an eye, and stopped singing immediately. The diamond on her finger was almost as bright as her smile.

*   *   *

He was filthy, but she was too thrilled to see him to obsess over the paint on his neck, the ring of job site dirt at his ankle. "Hi, bright eyes," she said, rinsing the shampoo from her hair. "Free for dinner?"

He pulled her into his arms and lowered his mouth to hers in a calculated, precise kiss, bubbles tickling down the backs of her legs. His arms enveloped her, squashing her breasts against his hot, muscled chest. Everything about his body was strength and power, and she smiled, knowing how it had come to be that way: hard work and dedication.

He tightened his grip around her, guiding her head to his shoulder. "I'm never going to let you go again." One of his hands pressed down along her spine and kissed her mouth, her neck, her eyes. "You belong here, kid. You belong with me."

One of his hands cupped her rear, lifting her, and she wrapped her legs around his waist. He was ready for sex. She could feel him hard against her, but he only held her more tightly with every passing second, kissed her tenderly, and caressed her wet skin.

His touch set her on fire; he wasn't the only one ready. But no matter how flagrant her response to his touch, he showed no sign of losing control. Every inch of her flesh craved him, and just knowing he wanted her made her want him more. "I missed you," she whispered in invitation.

"How much?" His smile toed the line between confidence and cockiness, and his thumb wiggled its way into the wet valley between her legs.

She gasped with the pleasure he brought, spiraling deeper and deeper into her. Involuntarily, she clenched his shoulders, her fingernails digging into his flesh and her mouth consuming his.

He pressed her against the sparkling white tile, slithering kisses down her neck to her breasts, rolling his tongue around her distended nipples, and sending shocks of pleasure throughout her entire body. She closed her eyes, breathing in staccato breaths.

It had been a mere ten days, but it seemed years had passed since she'd felt this good, this right, and she reached for him, determined to share the wealth of their love.

A groan hummed from deep in his throat, vibrating gently against her breasts, and he came up to meet her mouth again. "This one's all for you," he whispered against her lips. "Don't worry about me."

But she rolled her hips against him, denying his words and reaching for the red package she'd stashed in the soap dish. She bit it open, unrolled a condom over the length of him, and guided him to her opening.

A fervent sensation danced between her thighs, and the tip of his engorged penis probed her. She tightened her grip on his shoulders, the shower beating against their naked bodies as if they'd been caught in a rainstorm.

A millisecond later, he pushed into her, filling her with a thorough plunge. "Nicki Jeanne," he breathed at her neck.

Her thighs tensed against him, and she didn't have time to catch her breath. But she snapped her eyes open to find his brilliant, periwinkle stare settled on her.

She felt the grind of his sex between her legs as he pumped inside her with thorough thrusts, never taking his eyes from hers. Their noses brushed against one another, and he bit her mouth in an open-eyed, open-lipped kiss.

Deeper and deeper he burrowed into her flesh, and tighter and tighter she grasped.

His heart beat fiercely; she felt it reverberating against her body, and inside it, too. He was inside her in more ways than one, making love to her with his heart, his body, and the windows to his soul—those gorgeous, bright eyes.

She quivered with the thought of becoming *one* with this man, in every possible sense, and found she couldn't stop shivering. Her tunnel tightened around his shaft, and she trembled against him, around him.

His tongue rippled against hers and she couldn't hold on any longer. He was more than inside her, he was *in* her, in every way she could imagine, physically, emotionally. Spiritually, artistically. Building, tingling in every nerve, bouncing from the heat of her core to the tips of her toes, and still, she gripped him tighter, her orgasm the gateway to forever, one instant of pleasure spiraling into another and another, until she couldn't hold him any tighter, couldn't breathe, couldn't see anything beyond the dilated pupils of his eyes.

And then she saw nothing but color, colors everywhere, screaming like a freight train of pleasure through her body, starting with the nub between her legs and climbing, climbing, soaring, and plummeting, and climbing higher still. Her cry of pleasure caught in her throat.

Half a second later, with the gush of his release, he closed his eyes, water flickering off his thick lashes. He brushed his thumb against her chin and traced the outline of her lips.

She breathed in a long, slow breath, blinking away the spray of the shower. He twitched inside her, as if awakening, ready to do it all again.

"My God, I love what you do to me," he whispered. He kissed her eyes closed and raked a thumb across her hard nipple. "I love what we do together."

"Ty—"

He kissed her to quiet her and whispered against her lips, "I love everything you are, everything you were, everything you're going to be."

*   *   *

Clad in a worn Diamond Custom Homes T-shirt, Nicki lay across his chest on their bed, her damp hair spilling about her face. He envisioned her in the same position after every sex-filled shower, falling across him in exhaustion, as if there were no place she'd rather be.

He played with her hair with one hand, aware of the envelope he held in the other. "I can't wait to tell Verna you're back. She's going to—"

"Oh, she knows."

"She knows?"

"Why do think it was suddenly such an emergency that you work on her sunroom? And right after work? Who do you think unlocked the door for me? Left me eight tomatoes and an onion?"

"The two of you planned this?"

"I asked her to keep you occupied while I settled back in. And naturally, she had some questions, so I told her about your dad, about how he helped get me here."

"Good ole dad really came through for us."

"You don't know the half of it."

"Well, you've earned the letter of commendation, that's for sure."

"Think I've earned the chance to drive your car?"

"I don't know."

"I'm not going to kill her, you know."

He shrugged. "No, but you might grind the gears."

"I won't grind the gears." She rolled her eyes. "I had a good teacher. He taught me all about the precious, standard H of the only car ever to win the Tiffany award for design. I know she's special. I get it already, but for the love of God, let me drive your beloved Betty."

He smiled. "All right, first thing tomorrow."

"Really?"

"On our way to work."

"Your dad's right about one thing. We really do make a great team."

"Ray thinks so, too. He'll hire you in a heartbeat. I owe him a secretary, but he'll have to settle for a designer."

"In a few weeks, I might be running the place. I have a pretty impressive recommendation under my belt."

He laced his fingers into hers and caressed the heirloom ring. "Just out of curiosity, do you have anything to do with my dad's visit in a few days?"

"Whatever gave you that idea?"

He looked again to the envelope in his hand. "Do you expect me to believe he's coming solely to see what future this letter holds?"

"Do you want to open it?"

"Yes." He shook his head. "No." He licked his lips and shrugged a shoulder. "I don't know."

"This is your business, not mine." She pushed up from her position. "I'll give you a minute."

"Oh, no, you don't." He caught her wrist and pulled her back to his chest.

"I have to stir the sauce."

"What, is it going to burn?"

"Maybe."

"So let it burn. This is your business, too."

"Still, you should—"

"If you don't mind, you open it."

She frowned and rolled onto the mattress. "Absolutely not."

"At least stay while I do it then."

When she looked back to him, her hair was a pool of golden curls around her beautiful face, her eyes as warm as a Florida sunset. "Ty, no matter what's in there, I'm ready to hear it. But are you?"

He nodded. "I already know what it says. Doesn't make it any easier to read it, though. She's a beautiful child. Who wouldn't want to claim her?"

"Well, maybe you're wrong. There's only one way to find out."

He opened the envelope without further delay and scanned through paragraphs of legalese. "It is the finding of the laboratory at Weston Regional," he read at the top of page two, "that the sample submitted by Tyler Donovan Carmichael does not match that of Mia Celeste Washington." He dropped the pages, his fingers numb. "No match."

He glanced at Nicki, who lounged on their bed a mere fifteen inches away, with a hand resting on her stomach. So he wasn't a father. He looked again to her abdomen. Not yet anyway. "She isn't mine."

"I'm sorry."

"No, I'm okay." He dragged a finger along her tummy. "You should be the mother of my babies anyway."

She breathed deeply, a small smile darting across her utterly kissable lips, looking ready to be drawn. But she had to stir the sauce, and he had a lifetime to draw her again, and again, and again.

"I didn't know how I was going to live without you," he whispered, tangling a damp tendril around a finger, brushing her chin with a thumb. "I thought I'd lost you. I thought when you went home, you'd—"

"Ty," she whispered, crawling toward him and giving him the type of slow, sweet kisses that signified eternity. "I am home."

"Yes," he said against her lips. "You are."

PENNY DAWN

All right, so who among us doesn't have a few demons to exorcise?

Penny Dawn began her writing career at the tender age of seven, before she realized it's impossible to be All Good, All the Time...at least in the religious sense (grinning like a Cheshire.) Romantic stories with passionate twists have since become this Good Girl's forte...and she unleashes her demons on paper, over and over and over again.

Penny Dawn holds a B.A. in history and English from Northern Illinois University and is presently pursuing her M. A. in Creative Writing at Seton Hill University, whose alumnae include spicy novelists Jacki King, Shannon Hollis, Suzanne Forster, Dana Marton, and others. When she isn't writing, Penny enjoys tap, ballet, and jazz dance, photography, physical fitness, and renovating her 1906 Victorian Lady with her husband and two daughters.

Drop by her website www.pennydawn.com to discuss all things decadent.

AMBER QUILL PRESS, LLC
THE GOLD STANDARD IN PUBLISHING

QUALITY BOOKS
IN BOTH PRINT AND ELECTRONIC FORMATS

ACTION/ADVENTURE

SCIENCE FICTION

MAINSTREAM

FANTASY

ROMANCE

HISTORICAL

YOUNG ADULT

SUSPENSE/THRILLER

PARANORMAL

MYSTERY

EROTICA

HORROR

WESTERN

NON-FICTION

AMBER QUILL PRESS, LLC
http://www.amberquill.com